THE REAL NEWS!

THE NEVER-BEFORE-TOLD STORIES OF DONALD TRUMP & FAKE NEWS!

JOHN BERNARD RUANE

A POST HILL PRESS BOOK

ISBN: 978-1-64293-013-9
ISBN (eBook): 978-1-64293-014-6

The Real News!
The Never-Before-Told Stories of
Donald Trump & Fake News!

Post Hill Press, LLC
New York • Nashville
posthillpress.com

Published in the United States of America

To my fifth-grade teacher, Carol Pasko, and all teachers who recognize, support, and encourage the individual talents of their students.

CONTENTS

FOREWORD

It was a watershed moment in American history.

On June 16, 2015, Donald J. Trump announced that he was going to run for President of the United States, and millions of Americans across the country broke out in laughter. He must be kidding! It's a joke! He's just trying to use a Presidential run to promote himself and his business, as he has done in the past.

Over the final six months of 2015, Trump not only proved it was no joke, but he also did not drop out, as so many had predicted. As a matter of fact, he was building momentum. Once the Republican nominee debates began on August 6, that became his launching pad, because he took center stage, literally. His style and attacks on his opponents drew tremendous interest in America. It wasn't so much because of great political debate that addressed the important issues of the day, but because it was good television. Many tuned in just to see who he would attack and how he would attack them. Jeb Bush became "Low Energy Jeb!" He called Marco Rubio "Little Marco!" Ted Cruz was labeled, "Lyin' Ted!" These were the type of actions usually reserved for the schoolyard playground with the bully picking on the weaker kids. And that's exactly who Donald Trump revealed himself to be—the big bad bully picking on his opponents. As childish as it seemed to many, it proved to be great theater! Love him or hate him, you had to watch. It became the most popular show on TV. The first debate broadcast on FOX News drew twenty-four million viewers. The next one on CNN, drew eighteen million. The problem was that the country's future was at stake.

Then, when he took his show on the road for speaking engagements in large venues across the country, they were packed with lines stretching out the door. Donald Trump certainly proved he had millions of Americans who wanted him to become the next President of the United States. They were the Trump Nation, the Trumpsters. But he also had those who would do anything to stop him, including many in the regular Republican Party, those proclaiming, "Never Trump!"

But the best TV was yet to come. After he won the Republican Party's nomination and squared off against the Democratic nominee, Hillary Clinton, even more people across the country had to tune in to see his shenanigans. *Saturday Night Live* had a grand time with those debates, with Alec Baldwin playing Trump and Kate McKinnon playing Clinton, creating their own must-see TV during the first segment each week of the long-running satirical comedy show.

On November 8, 2016, when Donald Trump shocked the world and won the Presidential election, television crews focused in on shots of Clinton supporters who were completely devastated. After all, that was the day that Hillary Clinton was absolutely certain that she would be voted in as the first woman President of the United States. Instead, she was sent back to New York to roam the forest and try to figure out, "What Happened?"

One thing that did happen was Donald J. Trump promoted and used the term *Fake News* to place doubt in the collective minds of many Americans about the mainstream media's reporting about him, while telling his own version of the story on Twitter. Fake News became an ever-present buzz word, dating back to when Trump first started running for the highest office in the land. Given Trump's statements, and the obvious agenda of some news organizations, anyone interested in the news was faced with a quandary: Is it Real News? Or is it Fake News?

Because his proclamation about the news had been widely accepted by his base supporters, it allowed Trump to call any negative report about him "Fake News!" and Trump Nation immediately accepted their political hero's dismissive admonishment. The truth is that *The King of the Comb Over* calls any negative reports about him "Fake News" and the few positive news reports or commentary about him real news. There's no question, he is a bit of a "Dr. Jekyll and Mr. Hyde" news critic.

And when he is attacked for his words, actions or decisions, the Donald of Trump does not sit passively by and accept it. In the style taught to him by his mentor, Roy Cohn, any time he is attacked, he counter-attacks, only far more aggressively. "Fake News! Fake News! Fake News!" tweets Trump. From one election came so many controversial stories that the American public really didn't know what to believe. Many Americans decided to just read, listen to, or watch the news that agreed with their opinions. It was easier, less frustrating.

From the day he stepped into the White House, President Trump has made life in America quite anxious for millions of Americans who don't know how to deal with this man who continues to break every rule in politics. So, during his second year in the Oval Office, while many Americans continue to struggle with an unpredictable President whom they fear, satire has become a popular outlet to relieve some of that stress and pressure. The beauty of satire is that the truth can be communicated in a humorous fashion, not only to educate the audience, but entertain them with stories that keep their interest, using both fact and fiction in a satirical mix that makes the truth clear; at least from the writer's point of view.

In *The Real News!* author John Bernard Ruane presents a compilation of satirical stories about Donald Trump and some of the famous media who cover and comment on him, which has helped determine what many Americans think about the 45th President of the United States. In the "Fake News" versus "Real News" debate, these stories have NEVER been reported by any news outlets, or the *Tweeter in Chief,* UNTIL NOW! Although these stories were not reported to the American public, our anonymous sources—who we believe may be the same anonymous sources used by some of the major news media—have each confirmed separate accounts of these reports.

So here ONLY, for the first time, you can read these exclusive stories, including an incredible never-before-told story about the Democratic Party's Secret Six who discovered President Trump's greatest weakness to gain his support on gun control; the most shocking political achievement in American history; the untold story of former President Barack Obama taking a flying leap off the Brooklyn Bridge; President Trump delivering on his bold "Fifth Avenue" campaign statement; The Donald's hope to become a real man after an encounter with a Blue Fairy; the inside story revealing Oprah Winfrey's final decision on running for President; a shocking protest by thousands of Donald Trump's base supporters angry about the President's harmful words; an inside look at the President watching the Sunday Morning news talking heads; the day in 2008 when Melania Trump warned America about her husband; and an increase of anger among national television news commentators due to President Trump's actions which led the Television News Emmy Awards to add a new category to honor the Most Outraged News Commentator.

In addition, a few stories about some of the titans of the news media have been woven in to address some of the controversies of the day, including an unscheduled fight that broke out, during a celebrity boxing match, between a popular and beautiful FOX News host and her MSNBC rival; why David Letterman moved to Netflix; and the untold story of a dangerous and memorable evening shared by Stephen Colbert and Jon Stewart.

So now, for the first time, here are the exclusive, never-before-told stories about Donald Trump and Fake News!

It's *The Real News!*

CHAPTER 1

DEMOCRATS DISCOVER DONALD TRUMP'S GREATEST WEAKNESS

Wave after wave of young, motivated high school and college students streamed down Pennsylvania Avenue headed toward their destination, the stage in front of the U.S. Capitol Building, to participate in a national gun protest event.

News helicopters and drones buzzed overhead, filming this historical moment in America. Thousands of Centennials, Generation Z, led a massive group of protestors, young and old, down the famed tree-lined avenue with the sound of an army of shuffling athletic shoes and chants from the impassioned youth ascending into the cool, cloud-scattered blue skies over Washington, D.C.

Saturday, March 24, 2018 was the day that would be forever known as the day millions of Americans joined together for the *March for Our Lives* to protest for better gun control legislation in America.

It was quite a scene! The kids marching, holding up colorful signs reading, "No Guns in My School!" "Protect the Kids Not Your Guns!" "Ban Assault Weapons!" They pumped their fists in unity with each slogan as they shouted out, "Better background checks!" "No one needs an assault rifle!" "More guns, more death!"

Such young faces should have been filled with hope and happiness at this precious time in their respective lives. Instead, they were a universal canvas of fear, anger, and anxiety. Thousands of iPhones were held up high, photographing and recording this moment, shared on social media for the world to see.

Following the St. Valentine's Day Massacre of 2018 at Marjory Stoneman Douglas High School in Parkland, Florida, the students in America decided that they had better take the lead on this issue or nothing would get done. So on Wednesday, March 14, students walked out of their schools for seventeen minutes on *National Student Walkout Day* to honor the seventeen victims in Parkland. Ten days later, marches were held all across the country for *March for Our Lives*, making it clear that those lawmakers who stood against this effort and new gun control legislation would be voted out of office. The call to action was to vote against any politician taking money from the National Rifle Association (NRA).

These kids were angry! They were passionate. They were determined to make a change in America with the hope of making schools, and society, safe again.

They had plenty of justification. Over a three-year period, there were 239 school shootings nationwide with 438 people shot and 138 killed. That horrific period began on December 14, 2014, when the Sandy Hook Elementary School massacre took place and twenty first graders and six adults were murdered by crazed gunman Adam Lanza, and ended on February 14, 2018, when seventeen were killed by troubled nineteen-year-old Nikolas Cruz at Marjory Stoneman Douglas High School.

After each shooting, news reports flowed. Americans became upset. Many of the Republicans in the United States Congress blamed the shootings on mental illness. Across the aisle, their Democratic counterparts called for stricter gun control laws and background checks. Each time, after the political rhetoric ended, no action was taken. No gun control laws were changed.

After each shooting, the outrage was seen, heard, and voiced across America. But within a few weeks after every shooting that received media coverage, the rage faded away and it was business as usual in America. The politicians funded by the NRA counted on it. For many of those politicians, their base voters were strong Second Amendment rights supporters, so there was no risk in them continuing to stand for gun freedom, even when young children were being murdered in schools. Gun rights proponents stood by their convictions that the shootings were not the fault of the guns.

"It's mental illness! It's society's fault! I need my guns," were the common and consistent messages heard after each shooting. In their minds, there was no correlation between these massacres and society selling guns, including assault rifles, so freely that it seemed anyone could buy one.

President Barack Obama made a valiant effort to address this highly-contentious issue when he made a very strong common-sense appeal to the country in a speech on January 5, 2016. Two days later, he followed that with a Town Hall, broadcast live to the nation on CNN, to address all of the questions and concerns of gun owners. It seemed that no matter what he said, all of the assurances he gave to gun owners in the audience that evening fell on deaf ears. They absolutely refused to believe him. Gun owners had been sold fear by the NRA. They believed that any concession on gun rights would be a slippery slope, leading to the loss of their weapons. Watching the gun owners' response to President Obama on CNN, many adults in America who supported stricter gun control felt completely frustrated, numb. What more could be done? Twenty third graders had been shot and killed and President Obama's common-sense appeal didn't seem to move the needle at all for Republicans, the NRA, and many gun owners.

So, more mass shootings occurred and the ebb and flow of anger rose and fell with each event. The biggest killings grabbed the biggest headlines and round-the-clock cable television news coverage. On October 1, 2017, from his hotel room at the Mandalay Bay Resort, Stephen Paddock opened fire on the crowd below him at the Route 91 Harvest Music Festival in Las Vegas, killing fifty-eight people. No change to the gun laws. On November 5, 2017, Devin Patrick Kelley walked into the First Baptist Church in Sutherland Springs, Texas, and killed twenty-seven people. No change! Twenty-eight people were killed at a Little Rock, Arkansas, night club on July 1, 2017. No change! Even when several Congressional Republicans were practicing to play in a charity baseball game, and Trump-hater James Hodgkinson showed up with an assault rifle, opened fire, and injured six of the GOP lawmakers, there was still no change to the gun laws!

Whereas the politicians in Washington weren't willing to make changes, individuals and corporations didn't need to pass a bill to address the issue. Walmart and Dick's Sporting Goods, began limiting the sale of firearms; no more assault rifles and no one under twenty-one could purchase a weapon. Private citizens, who had been gun owners and strong Second Amendment rights supporters, began posting videos on social media sites dismantling or chopping up their guns, refusing to be on the wrong side of an issue where kids were getting killed.

President Trump, a well-known ardent supporter of the NRA, found out very quickly that his previous go-to excuse, blaming "mental illness" as the culprit and not the guns, was no longer going to fly with those who were most at risk—the kids. The game changed after the St. Valentine's Day massacre of 2018. The kids were now taking the lead.

The GOP gun rights lawmakers in Washington, who had always counted on the rage of adult Americans petering out as they went back to their jobs and lives, could not predict how these protests, led by the kids, would play out. They were a wildcard group to be sure, which put fear into the minds of the Republican politicians, hoping to keep their Congressional seats. How long would their rage continue? How effective would they be on influencing voting Americans? Those were the questions being asked by both Democrats and Republicans as they looked toward future elections, which could not only decide which party would take over the majority vote in Congress, but also the success or failure of gun-control legislation.

In an attempt to quell the anger, President Trump tried *Listening Sessions* with State Governors and then a bipartisan group of Congressional leaders. Under the lights of the television cameras, he once again put on a show, claiming he would act and put into place new programs to improve background checks and get rid of bump stocks. Many were skeptical about Trump's claims to put his words into action.

However, one Democratic lawmaker, Representative Chris Murphy of Connecticut, saw the only viable path to success on this issue was getting Donald Trump's support.

"Mr. President, it's going to have to be you that bring the Republicans to the table on this because right now the gun lobby would stop it in its tracks," said Murphy at the *Listening Session.* Murphy may not have been the President's biggest fan, but he wouldn't deny Trump's power and influence, which he hoped to capitalize on.

So that was the question. How would the gun-control advocates gain the support of President Donald Trump, an ardent pro-gun-rights advocate, in order to put legislation into effect that would take the dangerous weapons off the streets and make America safer?

As the weeks passed, new gun-protest events were held, with the young organizers focusing on the vote during any and all future elections that could impact gun legislation. By the beginning of June, Democrats had a much clearer picture of the gun-control actions taken as a result of the Parkland massacre. There was some progress, but to many it looked like small measures to appease the protestors and quell some of the anger, while the Trump administration worked hard to pull America's attention off gun control and onto other issues, like the North Korea summit.

On the morning of Wednesday, June 6, six Congressional Democratic leaders met in the office of Senate Minority Leader Chuck Schumer to devise a more impactful gun-control strategy. The main objective was to somehow gain the support of the President, who—as Chris Murphy stated—could bring the Republicans to the table and make real changes in gun-control legislation. The Secret Six, as they liked to call themselves, sat around the square, brown coffee table with Senator Schumer in his comfortable, chocolate-brown, cotton-blend armchair to lead the meeting.

"Look, as long as the kids keep protesting and signing up all their friends to vote, the GOP will be nervous, and it may put us in a position where we can negotiate and ram a bill through Congress before the midterms even take place," said Schumer, with House Minority Leader Nancy Pelosi and Senate Minority Whip Dick Durbin sitting on the long, gold, velvet couch next to him, nodding in agreement.

"I don't know," said House Minority Whip Steny Hoyer, seated in the gold armchair directly across from Schumer. "I don't know that they will have the numbers in some of those key races to win. Isn't there something else we can do on a grander scale to scare the hell out of the GOP to motivate a vote?"

"GOP? What about Trump?" asked Senator Bernie Sanders, who always insisted on sitting on the brown Churchill dining chair kept in Schumer's office especially for the Senator from Vermont. "If we can convince him that they will lose the House and Senate, he'll negotiate. He wants to put this behind him before the midterms."

"Yeah, well that's not going to happen," said Pelosi, whose attention was suddenly distracted by a young boy entering the office, wearing a yellow-straw cowboy hat, blue flannel shirt, wrangler jeans, and brown-leather cowboy boots. "We are riding this wave of youth all the way to the polls this November. And hopefully, we can take back Congress."

The Secret Six Democrats looked at the young man, who couldn't have been older than nine, as he walked over to Schumer's other gold, velvet couch, hopped up, and sat back to watch Democracy in action. In his right hand, the young lad was holding a large red, white, and blue lollipop, which he quickly began to sample.

"Oh hello, young fellow," said California Representative Adam Schiff, the youngest politician in the room, sitting on the opposite end of the couch from the boy. "Are you lost?"

The little boy just shook his head. "No, it's Take Your Kid to Congress Day. My pop works downstairs. Thought I'd take a walk and see how things are done around here."

The six leaders looked a bit startled at this answer. Senator Schumer took charge and said, "I'll just get one of my staffers to take him back downstairs."

The little cowboy stopped licking his lollipop for a moment and looked directly at New York's Senior Senator. "Excuse me Senator, are you trying to throw me out of here?"

A laughed exploded in the room, the veteran politicians never expected a nine-year-old to conduct himself in such a manner, not to mention the fact he knew Schumer was a senator.

"I'd like to stay, thank you very much," he said, then began licking his round, delicious lollipop, which he then held out to Senator Durbin. "Want a taste?"

Durbin just laughed. "No thank you…uh."

"Leon."

"Leon. No thank you, Leon, but I appreciate the offer."

"Okay, well, if you change your mind," said Leon, pulling his sucker back to enjoy the sugary treat.

"Okay so look," said Schumer. "I think they have come up with some great slogans that seem to be catching on nationwide. The Die-In protest really made an impact."

Pelosi interjected, "The 'shame on you' chants! And 'we call BS!' I know that bothered them."

"Yes, but did it bother them enough to stop taking money from the NRA?" asked Hoyer.

"No!" said Sanders. "Might have given them a half a second of indigestion, but that's about it. I've got some indigestion. Had I mentioned that?"

Nancy Pelosi stood and walked to the opening next to Schumer's chair in order to address her fellow Democratic leaders. "There has to be something more we can do than chip away at the dignity and character of the President and GOP leaders."

"Dignity and character, that's funny," quipped Schiff, who had become a recognizable Democratic leader through news coverage of his statements on most of the key issues of the day.

"I really think Trump can drive this for us, but how do you get our tough-guy President to do the right thing?" asked Pelosi. "He thinks he's so macho, such a tough guy. How do you get a guy like that to support the things that are morally right if he won't do them because it will lose him support among the GOP, NRA, and big money donors?"

"Well first of all Nancy, Trump really believes arming teachers, citizens, and everyone else is the right thing to do," said Durbin, sipping from his favorite *Illinois*-logoed coffee mug. "So, let's make sure we are working under the correct premise here to begin this discussion."

"Okay," she said. "Then how do we get the big, bad, tough guy to do what we know is right, even if he really doesn't know it's right? Yet!"

Silence filled the Senator's office, the sound of Leon licking his lollipop bouncing off the walls, which drew the attention of Senator Durbin, who looked over as if he was having second thoughts about accepting Leon's offer.

"I know the answer to that," said Leon, as all eyes shifted toward the young man on the couch, whose legs weren't long enough to touch the floor.

"I'm sorry, you know the answer to what, Leon?" asked Durbin, who watched Leon reach out his sucker toward him again, only this time the Senior Senator from Illinois took a taste.

"Boy that's good! Thanks Leon," said Durbin.

"I know how to get a tough guy to do the right thing, to do what you want him to do," he said, as he adjusted his cowboy hat with his left hand and took another lick of his sucker.

Schumer stood and reached out to take the boy by his hand to lead him out of the office, "C'mon son, we have important work to do here."

Leon pulled his hand back and blurted out, "You call him a chicken!"

A universal look of bewilderment crossed the collective faces of the Secret Six.

"If there is one thing boys, especially boys who think they are tough, can't stand, it's to be called a chicken," Leon continued, clicking his cowboy boots together, feeling a bit giddy to share his idea. "You call him a chicken and he will do exactly what you want him to do. I know this for certain. On the playground at recess for our third-grade class, I watched Dominic Cangelosi's reaction to Joe Smoger, who wanted him to crawl from one end of the fence to the other. Now, that's not something Dominic would have ever done on his own. Quite frankly, the idea itself is embarrassing and Dominic is generally considered to be the toughest kid in the third grade. We don't really know if he's the toughest kid, but he talks and acts like he is, so no one challenges him. So good ol' Joe Smoger, our blonde-haired, blue-eyed football quarterback, decides he's going to make Dominic look bad without even throwing a punch."

All six senators were completely focused on Leon's story as Durbin leaned in for another sugary taste, with Schiff looking on wondering if he should sample the treat.

"So Joe says, 'I'll bet you can't crawl from one end of this fence to the other in less than ten seconds,'" Leon continued.

"Dominic tried to laugh it off. And that's when Joe dropped it on him. He said, 'What's wrong Dominic, chicken?' Then he started flapping his arms and walking like a chicken saying, 'bwok, bwok, bwok, bwok!' Well I have to tell you, I think the chicken walk bothered Dominic. I think the chicken arms pissed him off. But I know the 'bwok bwok' made him crazy and he was on his hands and knees so fast. You never saw a kid crawl that quickly in your life. All because of the 'bwok bwok.' You see what I'm saying?"

Once again silence filled the room, with only the sound of the air conditioning kicking on. A look of surprise took center stage.

"Holy crap!" said Hoyer. "I think this kid's got something here."

"Wait," said Schumer. "We challenge President Trump to change the gun laws and increase background checks."

"Yes," said Hoyer. "And the minute he makes an excuse...."

Leon interrupted, with arms bent and waving, "Bwok, bwok, bwok, bwok!"

"Wow!" said Durbin. "That's brilliant! We all know Trump conducts himself like he's still on the third-grade playground. Why didn't we think of this earlier?"

Pelosi chortled, "You know the second you call Trump chicken, he'll view that as a challenge to his manhood and he'll do whatever we want him to do."

"Tough guys hate the bwok bwok," said Leon, reaching out his lollipop so all in the room could celebrate and enjoy the sweet taste of a great idea.

Senator Schumer announced a press conference would take place that afternoon on the steps of the U.S. Capitol Building. At 5:00 p.m., all of the Congressional Democrats, forty-six senators and 191 Representatives, stood on the

Capitol steps behind Chuck Schumer and the Secret Six. It was a beautiful day in Washington, with the sun still bright as Schumer prepared his notes at a tall, brown, wooden podium with the round red, white, and blue United States Congress emblem on the front of it. Nancy Pelosi and Adam Schiff stood on his right and Durbin, Hoyer, and Sanders stood to his left. Leon stood in front of the podium, holding his half-eaten lollipop.

Every major news organization was positioned in front of the Senator ready to record and broadcast his address live. No one had been tipped off to the specifics of his speech, just that Senator Schumer had a very important announcement to make.

Back at the White House, President Trump sat with Vice President Mike Pence and NRA Executive Vice President Wayne LaPierre at a beautiful, hand-carved mahogany table, in the dining room where the President often eats his lunch among stacks of newspapers and briefing documents. Above them was a large, beautiful, glass chandelier, which Trump paid for with his own money. On the wall across from them was a fireplace with a large, sixty-inch flat screen television above it and FOX News tuned in to watch Schumer's speech.

"Pencey, what do you know about this talk that Fake Tears Chuck is about to give?" asked the President.

"Not much Mr. President," responded the white-haired wonder from Indiana. "We have tried everyone, but no one seems to know anything."

"Not even our Democratic spies?" asked Trump.

"All they could say was that there is a group of senators called the Secret Six who were behind this and they were keeping it top secret."

LaPierre interrupted them, "He's about to speak."

Trump picked up his gold-plated, Trump-logoed channel controller, pointed it toward the television, and turned up the volume.

Senator Schumer looked at the papers in front of him with his typed remarks and began, "I want to thank all of you for coming here today on such short notice. Today marks an important day in our country's history. We chose D-Day because we believe it is quite appropriate given the war on guns being waged in this country. Our Democratic leadership just concluded a meeting where we drafted the basis of legislation that will ban all assault rifles throughout the United States. All of them! This legislation will limit gun sales to those over twenty-one years of age and create very strict background checks for anyone purchasing any firearm in the United States. This will make it difficult, if not impossible, for anyone who has any behavioral issue, including any mental health history or drug and alcohol abuse, to purchase a gun.

"One aspect of this debate we fully agree upon with our GOP leaders is that mental health and all behavioral health issues need to be a red flag on gun sales. In addition, gun shows will no longer be allowed to take place in America! Internet sales of weapons in the Fifty States will end. This will be monitored and managed by the FBI, so there is no way to get around it. From this point forward, once this bill has passed, the United States government will take control of managing the guns in this country and keeping our citizens safe. Citizens will still be able to have pistols to defend themselves and hunting rifles for sport. We are not taking away the Second Amendment. Now I will take your questions."

In the White House dining room, President Trump, LaPierre, and Pence just started laughing. "Is he kidding?" asked Trump. "Is this some kind of a joke?"

"Well it's not April Fool's Day," said Pence, shaking his head back and forth in disbelief. "So I don't know what he is trying to do here."

At the Capitol, several dozen reporters' hands were raised, hoping to get the first question. Schumer, who would have normally chosen a reporter from one of the three major networks, purposely pointed to FOX News reporter, John Roberts.

"Senator Schumer, with all due respect," began the salt-and-pepper-haired veteran White House correspondent. "What makes you and your Democratic colleagues believe that any of those gun control proposals will pass through a Congress with a Republican majority?"

Trump laughed and slapped LaPierre on the back, "That's what I'd like to know, eh Wayne. Seriously, has Schumer lost his mind?"

The Democrats standing behind Schumer leaned in to hear his response, because they most certainly were wondering the same thing. Schumer just looked to his left at the smiling Pelosi and Schiff and then to his right at Durbin, Hoyer, and Sanders.

"I'll tell you why this legislation, every line of it, will pass through Congress," said a smiling Schumer, looking down at Leon, who was nodding his head while licking his lollipop. "Because our President, Donald J. Trump, will take the lead on this and get it passed with the GOP in both the House and Senate. Every line of it. Every word of it. Representative Chris Murphy was right about that and we were listening."

Roberts and everyone else on the Capitol steps looked at the Secret Six wondering if they were trying to make a joke, or if they had seriously lost their collective minds.

"Senator Schumer, as you know the President is a strong supporter of the Second Amendment and the NRA," Roberts followed up. "What makes you think he will change his position on this incredibly divisive issue and help you get this gun control legislation passed?"

Schumer just smiled again, nodded to Leon, "I'll tell you why John, because Donald Trump will not let the Republicans in Congress tell him what to do."

"No, I won't," said Trump. "Won't do that."

"Donald Trump will not let the NRA tell him what to do," said Schumer.

"Nope NRA won't dictate my policy," said Trump, looking at LaPierre who suddenly had a look of concern cross his face.

"I think everyone here knows that Donald Trump is a tough guy, a real tough guy, and will not let the NRA and Republicans push him around any longer," continued Schumer.

"I'm tough, very tough guy," said Trump. "Schumer knows it. Everyone knows it."

"Because if this bill went no-where, it would only mean that our President, Donald J. Trump, kowtowed to the NRA!" Schumer said, slamming his fist on the podium.

"Kowtow? I don't kowtow for anyone!" yelled Trump.

"It would mean, and I say this with the greatest of respect," said Schumer, his voice dropping a bit, and then bellowed out, "That Donald Trump is a chicken!"

Trump shot to his feet, "What!"

The photographers' shutters on their cameras went berserk capturing the leading Democrat calling the President of the United States, 'Chicken.'

"Chicken!" said Trump. "Did he just call me a chicken?"

"Yes, he did Mr. President, chicken!" said Pence.

"Shut up, Pency!" Trump demanded.

"I'm no chicken!" Trump said as he paced back and forth in front of the flat screen television, getting angrier with each step, then turned and glared at LaPierre. "You think I'm afraid of you Wayne?"

"I didn't say anything Mr. President," said LaPierre, who all of a sudden felt like the kid getting picked on by the bully on the playground. He stood slowly and said, "Look Mr. President, they are obviously just trying to get under your skin here…"

Just then their attention was turned back to the flat screen and Schumer.

"Today, we call on President Trump as leader of this nation to join us on this legislation for stricter gun control and background checks," said Schumer. "We know that he is very interested in this effort, because he won't be pushed around any longer by the NRA. No, I think the last thing in the world President Donald Trump wants to do is admit that he is a chicken."

"There it is again," said Trump. "He's calling me a chicken. Why if I was down there, I'd knock his head off."

"But he's not the one calling you a chicken," said Pence. "He's saying that Wayne here and the NRA are calling you a chicken."

Trump violently threw the dining room chair to the side and walked toward the NRA leader, "Is that right Wayne? Is that right LaPierre? Are you calling me a chicken?" asked Trump in a threatening tone, getting right up into the face of the NRA leader.

"No sir," LaPierre said, quickly backing up from the angry President. "I would never call you a chicken."

"Schumer says you did," Trump yelled at him.

Schumer continued, “The NRA thinks Donald Trump is too chicken to join us in this very important legislation. And, just so the country understands what we are saying here, we don’t want to see our President act like a…Leon.”

The nine-year-old boy in his cowboy hat began strutting his chicken walk in front of the podium, flapping his bent elbows and saying, “Bwok, bwok, bwok! Bwok, bwok, bwok, bwok!”

Trump’s jaw dropped. He walked directly in front of the television, “Is he bwoking at me like I’m a chicken? Is that what that kid is doing? The chicken walk with the chicken bwok!”

LaPierre tried to calm down the now red-faced President, who had sweat pouring down his entire face, “Sir please understand the NRA is behind you, one hundred percent. Remember, we gave you thirty million dollars.”

“Yeah, you thought you could buy me off cause I’m such a chicken!” Trump shouted at the NRA leader. “Well I’m no chicken, LaPierre. And I hate the bwok bwok.”

Once again Schumer spoke into the microphone, “Because Mr. President, I think the last thing in the world you want to see is an entire country looking at you and doing this.” He then turned to the 237 Democrats behind him, each of whom put on a red ‘Make America Great’ cap, and then started doing the chicken walk, flapping their elbows and screaming out, “Bwok, bwok, bwok!!”

Trump, completely overcome by the sight of couple hundred Democratic lawmakers strutting back and forth like chickens, basically calling him a chicken, fainted and fell hard to the brown-carpeted dining room floor. LaPierre and Pence just watched in horror, the Vice President quickly rushing to the side of Trump, “Call an ambulance!” shouted Pence.

LaPierre scurried to the door, realizing this was his opportunity to get away before the schoolyard bully was revived.

This was an incredible scene in Washington, D.C. In the White House, the Vice President knelt over his fallen President who was out cold, but breathing, while four Secret Service agents and several medical personnel rushed through the door with a power stretcher to wheel the President off to an awaiting ambulance for the quick ride to Walter Reed Medical Center. A few minutes later, as the ambulance passed the U.S. Capitol, pandemonium continued on the steps with not only the Democrats doing the chicken dance, but the thousands of spectators in the area who had witnessed the press conference, joining in on the fun. The television news cameras and photographers moved around the large crowd, all watching and following the lead of a nine-year-old little boy in the cowboy outfit, licking his lollipop, flapping his arms, and shouting out, "Bwok, bwok, bwok, bwok!"

The Secret Six—Schumer, Pelosi, Durbin, Hoyer, Schiff, and Sanders—just stood there, marveling at the young man who came up with the idea that could possibly bring real gun control legislation to a country that so desperately needed it for the safety of all, but especially the kids.

Schumer made one final comment during a live shot on CNN, when asked by Anderson Cooper, "Do you really think any of this will make a difference in the gun-control legislation?"

Schumer just smiled, looked down at his pal Leon standing next to him, and said, "Sometimes, it takes a third-grade mentality to figure out how to deal with a third-grade tough guy on the playground. Right, Leon?"

"Yep!" said Leon, lifting his lollipop toward the CNN camera to offer America a taste.

CHAPTER 2

THE MOST SHOCKING POLITICAL ACHIEVEMENT IN AMERICAN HISTORY

Over the history of American Presidential campaigns, there have been many amazing, unbelievable political accomplishments that have been achieved. Accomplishments that for many seemed impossible, unimaginable, and entirely unpredictable!

In 1844, an unknown former congressman and governor of Tennessee, James K. Polk, upset former President Martin Van Buren in the primary to become the Democratic nominee. Polk then went on to defeat Whig Party candidate Henry Clay and became the 11th President of the United States. This was an incredible victory for Polk!

In the 1948 Presidential race, Thomas Dewey was proclaimed the winner by the *Chicago Daily Tribune*'s headline, "Dewey Defeats Truman." However, that turned out to be Fake News and "Give 'em Hell, Harry" stayed in the office he had been filling since four-term President Franklin Delano Roosevelt passed in April of 1945. Big win for the man who dropped the big bomb that ended World War II.

In 1960, another unknown candidate, a World War II hero from a wealthy family in Massachusetts, Senator John Fitzgerald Kennedy, defeated powerful and well-known Texas Senator, Lyndon Baines Johnson, in the Democratic primary. He then went on to defeat former Vice President Richard Milhous Nixon by only 0.17 percent of the popular-vote, the closest margin of the twentieth century.

Incredible achievements all! But, of all the mind-boggling political achievements that have taken place in American history, perhaps none is more incredible, more unimaginable, than the election on November 8, 2016—the day Donald J. Trump won the Presidency of the United States.

Certainly Mr. Trump didn't win the election due to overwhelming excitement for him and his potential as the Commander in Chief of the United States. A large percentage of the sixty-three million who punched a hole in the box next to his name didn't actually vote for Trump, but against his Democratic opponent, Hillary Clinton. The *Nose-Holding* never-Hillary voting group sealed the election for Donald Trump, which may be remembered for having the highest number of *Nose-Holder* voters in American political history. Once that election nightmare was ended and *Crooked Hillary* was sent back to upstate New York, the *Nose-Holders* hoped and prayed the new President, Trump, would actually do some of the things he promised without getting America into a nuclear war. Bringing back jobs to the United States as well as adding conservative judges to the Supreme Court were at the top of the list for many of the *Nose-Holders*, a group of voters mostly comprised of moderate conservatives and independents.

After completion of his first year in office, Americans were able to push aside the three-ring circus led by ringmaster Donald, and look at the facts—his record. Besides driving liberals crazy, what did President Donald Trump actually achieve during his first year in office?

Certainly, he should get credit for sparking the economy, with the stock market reaching record highs. Unemployment fell from 4.8 percent to 4.1 percent. Bringing jobs back to America was still in question, but the Republicans believed the GOP tax bill signed off by President Trump on December 22, 2017, would be the key to bringing back jobs from overseas. For his promise to appoint conservative judges, he was successful in sending Neil Gorsuch to the Supreme Court, while setting a record for confirming the most federal appeals judges during the first year of a presidency. Terrorism? U.S. Secretary of Defense, James "Mad Dog" Mattis, led the U.S. military and put ISIS and Al-Qaeda on the run in the Middle East, decimating their forces with multiple ground operations and air strikes. And, after battles with courts and judges trying to stop him regarding a very contentious issue, the Trump administration claimed a win for the travel ban on six Muslim-majority countries, their citizens no longer allowed to enter the United States for fear of terrorism. Trump also claimed victory for cutting regulations including net neutrality and environmental rules.

In the losing column, Trump and the GOP-held Congress were unable to repeal and replace Obamacare, one of his major campaign promises. Plans to build the 'Trump Wall' along the Mexican border had not moved forward and Mexican leaders laughed at his suggestion that they would pay for it. Trump was less than polite with many foreign leaders and was playing hardball with North Korea, which looked like a very dangerous game at the end of his first year in office.

However, into his second year, he made great progress, and if he were to achieve denuclearization of North Korea, that would be a remarkable accomplishment. Meanwhile, immigration reform here remained a heated battle with Deferred Action for Childhood Arrivals (DACA) as the centerpiece, trying to be fair to those immigrants who were brought to America as children, while his continuing rhetoric dismissed and offended Hispanics as a group.

There are many more, but in general, Donald Trump's first year as President can be accurately described as a year of achievement and great turmoil, offending or angering nearly everyone, while at the same time, making progress on some of his campaign promises. It's on the record. At the end of his first year, a number of the best pollsters in the land checked the approval for the President and the consensus was that one in four, roughly 24 percent of the voting public, still supported Trump.

It's true. Despite the continuing litany of lies, the flip-flops, the bad behavior, the name-calling, the sexual offense allegations, sympathizing with neo-Nazis, documented adultery with a porn star, offensive remarks to foreign leaders, deregulation of everything, and environmental irresponsibility, there are potentially forty million Americans who continue to support President Trump.

Of that forty million, some of the *Nose-Holders* who checked the box next to Trump's name on the ballot, are still on-board, still holding their nose, as they watch, hoping this challenging President will have the opportunity to nominate another Supreme Court Justice, as well as bring back jobs to America. They aren't ardent Trump supporters, but mostly never-Hillary Americans stuck with the only other choice, who may just deliver on a few of his major campaign promises that are important to them.

But the base supporters, the true supporters for the man called Trump, are the greatest mystery in America. Trump's loyalists are those who will stand behind him on Fifth Avenue, or anywhere else he feels like shooting someone. This is the angriest group in America, who love Trump's defiance, his tweets, his insults, and dismiss all negative commentary about their heroic President. The rest of America looks at Donald Trump's base, the Trumpsters, with great curiosity, wondering how they can be so vehemently supportive of a Vietnam hero-bashing, caught-on-camera misogynist, racist, and bigot-encouraging playground bully.

To answer this question, the *Nose-Holders of America* were able to get a government grant and commissioned a study on the Trumpsters, forming an investigative committee called the *What the Hell is Wrong with You? Council.* Yes, this group was tasked with identifying a top research group and lead investigator who could conduct a thorough study of the Trumpsters, who seem quite *Trumpitized,* living in their own world, known as *Trump Nation.*

After minutes of searching, the council enlisted the services of Dr. Victor Von Schnitzengruben from the Melbrooksian Institute to conduct a study of 500 hard-core Donald Trump supporters to understand why they continued supporting the man without any reservation for his conduct.

The study protocol, developed by Dr. Von Schnitzengruben, included both physical and mental examinations conducted over a ten-day period. In the first physical test, the 500 study subjects were handed a stick of Wrigley spearmint gum and asked to place the gum into their mouth and chew it. Then, they were asked to walk twenty-five yards, while chewing the gum, then turn directly around and see if they could find their way back to the starting line. Of the twenty-five who made it back to the starting line, only five were identified to have successfully walked and chewed gum at the same time.

In another study examination, recipients were asked to stand in front of a large, two-foot-deep hole in the ground. Then they were asked to bend over and place their head between their legs. Of the 500 study subjects, only six were able to correctly identify the difference between their ass and the hole in the ground.

For the final physical test, each was given a coloring book and asked to color inside the lines of the Donald Trump drawing, and then the Hillary Clinton figure. Whereas 99 percent were able to color inside the lines very neatly for the Trump drawing, none were able to color inside the lines for Hillary; most electing to write profane messages in bright red crayon all over the page. From that coloring book data, Dr. Von Schnitzengruben concluded that the study subjects loved Donald Trump but hated Hillary Clinton.

"Brilliant!" said Mac McDougal, Chairman of the *What the Hell is Wrong with You? Council.* "Who could have ever guessed that was the case without the coloring book research? So glad we commissioned this study."

Perhaps the greatest revelations came upon further mental examination of 100 selected study subjects, who agreed to a biopsy of their brains. The biopsies conclusively showed that more than half of the subjects had traces of manure in their brains. This information came as somewhat of a shock to the scientists, as well as a former Trump campaign manager who preferred to speak anonymously about this revolutionary research.

"Look, we suspected for years that a large number of our base supporters had shit for brains, but now it has been confirmed," said the former Trump campaign manager. "For example, we had tried for several months to figure out why anyone would believe Donald Trump when any third-grade kid could tell you that he lies all the time and never admits he's wrong. We could never figure it out. But now, this revelation about his base supporters having shit for brains is really helpful in our understanding of how we got anyone, and I mean anyone, to vote for this moron."

Of the sixty-two found with traces of manure in their brains further questioning was conducted. This portion of the study focused on reading and news habits, which revealed:

- Of the 500 in the study, 40 percent did not attend college and had not read a book since leaving high school. Of that 40 percent, half dropped out of high school.
- Seventy-five percent of that group said they read several news publications to keep up to date including *Breitbart News and The National Enquirer*.

Dr. Von Schnitzengruben explained these findings saying, "This is a group that hates elitist liberals, hates them with a passion. From the data, it's obvious that some of them do value education, whereas many do not and are quite comfortable with their work and lifestyles. When I pressed them about not being able to walk and chew gum at the same time, or not knowing their ass from a hole in the ground, that didn't seem to bother them. When I asked them how they could support a foul-mouthed, offensive President, the most common answer was a quickly raised middle finger, followed by an invitation to 'Suck it!' Yes, I believe that's how they put it. They were very clear on the 'Suck it!' information. They seemed to take great delight in communicating this to us and repeated it several times while doing a little dance to emphasize their point and belittle us as much as possible."

Von Schnitzengruben left that day believing he had made a breakthrough with his study and was eager to publish it. On his way back to the Melbrooksian Institute, he received an urgent call from one of his research associates, who informed him that they had received the results for the study extension that asked the Trumpsters specific political questions.

"They would answer the questions with a very angry tone, using each question as an opportunity to rail against foreigners or support building a wall," said Mr. Nathaniel Lane, one of the lead producers in the research project. "We could see that we were not going to get any legitimate answers, so we went to plan B, attempting to do the biopsy on their brains."

"And did that work?" asked Dr. Von Schnitzengruben.

"Well, we were able to do biopsies on about half of the one hundred subjects," explained his associate.

"And was there a trace of manure?"

"No. They were each packed with manure."

"Oh my goodness, are you saying…"

"Yes, they were all full of shit!"

"Well, I have to say, that makes sense," said Von Schnitzengruben. "What about the other fifty in the study?"

"We couldn't get to their brains because every one of those Trump supporters was walking around with their head up their ass."

"Oh, I see," said a dejected Von Schnitzengruben, hoping for better news. "Well, did you at least have the chance to ask them if they would have continued supporting Trump if he had shot someone on Fifth Avenue."

"Yes, we did. And there was one hundred percent agreement on this question, saying they would not only support Trump, but give him the hardware to level the bastards if they were liberals or commies."

"Well thank you Mr. Lane, I'll include that information with our research results for our client."

A few weeks later, Dr. Von Schnitzengruben and Mac McDougal appeared on MSNBC's *Morning Joe* and *FOX and Friends* to present the results of the ground-breaking study to both a liberal and conservative audience on national television. Shortly afterwards, the government grant received by the *What the Hell is Wrong with You? Council* was cut with no explanation.

Interestingly enough, President Trump tweeted shortly afterwards, writing, "No one knocks my base supporters. They're the best! Walking and chewing gum at the same time is over-rated. How many liberals know their ass from a hole in the ground? Huh?"

CHAPTER 3

OBAMA TAKES FLYING LEAP OFF BROOKLYN BRIDGE

The clock struck 6:30 p.m. on this Wednesday and the familiar musical opening to the *CBS Evening News* was being broadcast on the Times Square Jumbotron as thousands of New Yorkers below hurried to catch their train or bus out of Manhattan. A few tourists looked up to see the Tiffany Network's new anchor, Jeff Glor, introduce the night's most urgent news.

"President Trump warns North Korea to end their nuclear missile development or he will blow the S.... out of their S-hole country," began Glor, refraining from using the full curse word to meet CBS standards and practices guidelines. "President Trump dug the first ceremonial shovel full of dirt to begin the start of the wall along the Mexican border, saying he knows more about digging shovels full of dirt than anyone. But first, we have an exclusive live report about the repair and improvement of the Brooklyn Bridge, where our Nancy Cordes is standing."

On the screen appeared CBS veteran political reporter Nancy Cordes, dressed in her warm, black, Eddie Bauer, hooded down parka, holding a branded CBS microphone, while a gusty wind was having its way with her beautiful, shoulder-length, brunette hair.

"Thanks Jeff. Yes, I'm here on the second deck of the Brooklyn Bridge to report on the integrity of the girders that keep this bridge upright and operational, and have held it up since 1870," said Cordes, looking somewhat awkward giving her report. "Now if we can just pan over to this large girder here, where you can obviously see the East River behind it…."

Just then, a man came flying down from the first deck, into the camera shot and straight down toward the East River. "Oh my God! Did you see that, Jeff?"

A two-shot appeared on the screen with Jeff Glor at the anchor desk and Cordes shown running over to the side of the bridge. As the veteran newswoman reached the guard rail, the same man who was seen plummeting to the river was once again seen in the camera shot; this time flying back upwards as Cordes's head snapped back to watch him ascend to the first deck of the bridge.

"Oh my God!" exclaimed Cordes, then turned to her cameraman. "Jim, did you get a shot of that?"

The camera shot moved up and down twice, as if Jim the cameraman was nodding that he did indeed get the shot.

Jeff Glor interrupted, "Nancy, that looks like someone is bungee jumping off the side of the Brooklyn Bridge. Is that right?"

"Yes, Jeff, it is definitely bungee jumping," she confirmed. "But I have a very good view and that's not just *someone* bungee jumping off the Brooklyn Bridge. I believe that is none other than Steve Bannon. Jim, isn't that who it looked like to you?"

Again, the camera shot moved up and down twice.

"Jim says yes."

"Yes, we get it, Nancy. Thanks for translating," said Glor, a bit sarcastically, as another person was seen flying down through the camera shot and toward the river. Cordes looked over, "Now that's someone else, Jeff. That was not Steve Bannon that time. I could tell because whoever that person is actually shaved and had a neat haircut."

"So definitely not Bannon," quipped Glor, "That's for sure."

"Oh, here he comes back up," said Cordes, as her eyes grew wide seeing the man coming toward her.

"Oh my God, I'm not certain," she said, sounding a bit stunned. "Yes, I think it is. Here, let me see if I can get a quick interview."

As the man came flying back up and into the camera shot, Cordes shouted out, "President Obama, why are you bungee jumping off the Brooklyn Bridge?"

Obama's voice could barely be heard coming over the CBS sound system when he said, "I'm responding to all the GOP appeals for me to go take a flying leap…"

Jeff Glor came back on, "What? Who did you just say that was?"

"That was definitely the former President of the United States, Barack Obama, who apparently feels an obligation to fulfill the requests made by some of his opponents during his time as President."

"You've got to be kidding me?" Glor laughed.

"No, that was definitely him and I do believe the first man was Steve Bannon, but I would have to see him again," she said, looking up. "Oh wait, there are two people coming down simultaneously this time. Here they come! Jim, make sure you get this shot."

She stepped back as the camera showed two men flying down through the camera shot and toward the river.

"No question about it, Jeff, that was Barack Obama bungee jumping with Steve Bannon. That's something you don't see every day. And it's exclusive, right here on CBS."

The two men were seen flying back up as Cordes shouted out, "Hey, do you guys go bungee jumping together a lot…? No answer, Jeff. They must have been busy trying to avoid hitting their heads on a girder, so they wouldn't be killed."

"That's kind of understandable," said Glor. "Nancy, I have to tell you this is one of the strangest stories we have ever reported here on the *CBS Evening News.* This really looks like a story that would appeal to those between the ages of eighteen and thirty-four, but that's just a guess in case anyone at home knows of people that age and would like to invite them to watch this very exciting story."

Back in Times Square, a large crowd of people had stopped to watch the exclusive story being reported by CBS. Nearly everyone had their iPhones out and were recording it then sharing it on social media.

With the two-shot on the screen, all of a sudden someone else came flying down through the camera shot. "Nancy, I think that was a woman that just flew down," said Glor, while Cordes ran to the side to see who had jumped.

"Oh my goodness," she said. "That was a woman Jeff. And not just any woman, but the greatest female politician in the history of the United States!"

"Sarah Palin?" quipped Glor, always the comedian.

"No, Hillary Rodham Clinton! Here she comes," said Cordes, then shouted out loudly, "Secretary Clinton, do you have any comments about why you are bungee jumping today with Steve Bannon and Barack Obama?" The reporter watched Clinton ascend back up to the first deck, where her voice could be heard as she responded loudly, "I should have won that damn election, that's why!"

Cordes turned to the camera and seemingly with a chip on her shoulder said, "She should have won the election. She really should have."

"Thanks Nancy, certainly no apparent bias there," said Glor, injecting his deadpan dry humor. Just then, another person flew down through the camera.

"And one more thing, Jeff…."

"Sorry to interrupt you Nancy, but who was that?" asked Glor.

Cordes looked down, "Well, that's none other than Kate Winslet. Wait, here she comes. Kate, why are you bungee jumping with Barack Obama, Steve Bannon, and Hillary?"

"Seems like a normal everyday question to me," Glor chimed in.

The cameraman was able to get a great shot of her coming back up and as she drew closer to Cordes and the cameraman, she shouted out, "See *Titanic* in a theater near you to celebrate the twentieth anniversary!" She then flew up and onto the first deck.

"Boy, that seemed a little odd," said Glor. "Almost like it was a promotion for *Titanic*. I think we do need to mention that the same company that owns us owns Paramount Pictures, which is re-releasing *Titanic* on the big screen beginning this Friday. But that's just a complete coincidence."

Cordes was shown looking up and said, "I think they are done bungee jumping, Jeff. But I can say for certain, we are the only network that has this story, real news, right here on the *CBS Evening News!*"

The director cut back to Jeff Glor in the studio who said, "Well thank you, Nancy, for that in-depth report on the repair of the Brooklyn Bridge girders and the exclusive report on the bungee jumpers. Let me just say hello to all of our fans in Times Square."

The now very large crowd looking up at the Jumbotron began cheering wildly, as a CBS camera had been positioned there and a shot of the cheering crowd appeared on the evening news and the Jumbotron.

At FOX News, Sean Hannity was sitting at his desk, watching the report by Cordes and noticed something different about President Obama. He immediately picked up the phone to make an urgent call, and after a quick conversation, bolted out the door. Fifteen minutes later, his network's news broadcast returned from a commercial break.

"Hello and welcome back to *Special Report*, we have a breaking news story to report," said FOX News anchor Bret Baier. "We have sent our own Sean Hannity to the Brooklyn Bridge to cover this story. Sean."

"Thanks, Bret," said Hannity, dressed in a tan trench coat with the camera shot showing a group of people over his shoulder. "Yes, when we arrived here, we had expected to find Steve Bannon, Barack Obama, Hillary Clinton, and Kate Winslet standing here after bungee jumping off the Brooklyn Bridge, which is what CBS has been reporting exclusively tonight. If that report were true, or real news, our hope was to interview them about why they all chose to go bungee jumping together.

"But as I watched the report and saw former President Obama hurtling toward the East River at over a hundred miles per hour—a moment that I'm sure puts a smile on the collective faces of many of our FOX viewers—I noticed something different about him, which led me to believe that this may be Fake News. Now Bret, as you can see, as our cameraman Paul zooms in on the group of people behind me, you see four people who look somewhat like Bannon, Obama, Clinton, and Winslet with a hair and makeup artist carefully taking off their makeup. Now we are going to walk over to them and as we get closer, you can see that these are not the people we thought they were."

Hannity approached the African-American man in a nicely tailored blue suit who somewhat resembled Obama, but as the makeup came off, not so much.

"Hello sir, I'm Sean Hannity of FOX News," said the well-known commentator who had established himself as President Donald Trump's greatest supporter, and possibly best friend. "Can you tell me what you four are doing here tonight?"

"Bungee jumping!" said the man, quite excited.

"Yes, we know, but why are you bungee jumping?" asked Hannity.

"Well, we are all actors and were cast in a new show CBS is producing. I play President Barack Obama. That's Hillary Clinton over there. There's Steve Bannon and Kate Winslet."

Hannity took one look at the Kate Winslet character and said, "Now wait a minute, you really are Kate Winslet."

The famous British actress smiled, "Yes, I'm here to promote the re-release of *Titanic* on the big screen at theaters across the country. It's this weekend for all your viewers, if they want to experience it like the first time they saw it. And

I'll be making appearances at some of the theaters, so there's a chance people in your audience will see me."

"Yeah, sure they will, Kate," said Hannity sarcastically, realizing Winslet was spewing her own brand of Fake News. "But do you realize what you have all done here? Yes or no!"

The actress looked a bit stunned at the aggressive tone of the question.

"Yes or no!" continued Hannity. "Do you realize that what you have presented as breaking news by the *CBS Evening News* is Fake News? Yes or no! Just answer the question. Yes or no!"

The actress playing Hillary Clinton stepped into the shot, "Well of course it's breaking news. I'm Hillary Rodham Clinton and I should have won that election. And the only way to make that clear to all of America is by bungee jumping off the Brooklyn Bridge. Am I right?"

"No," said Hannity. "You're wrong! This is Fake News! Literally completely made up with a movie promotion thrown in to boot. But thank you for your time."

Hannity then turned back to the camera, "Bret, we have just uncovered our own exclusive here today. CBS creating Fake News in an attempt to draw higher ratings with viewers eighteen to thirty-four while they push the re-release of a movie owned by their parent company."

Bret Baier appeared back on the screen laughing, "Sean, how did you know that this might be a Fake News story?"

"Well, I was sitting in the newsroom, watching the report, and noticed that Barack Obama's ears were normal size. The entire world knows that the former President's ears are unusually large and if he were actually falling toward the East River, one would assume that he would start flapping those head-wings like nobody's business to try and fly."

"You mean like Dumbo?" asked Baier.

"Well, yes, like Dumbo the elephant," said a smirking Hannity, appreciative of his anchor's analogy.

Just then, another FOX News truck came screaming around the corner with President Donald Trump standing on the running board on the right side of the vehicle, hanging onto the mirror with his left hand, and pointing at the CBS crew with his right hand, yelling out, "Fake News! CBS Fake News!"

The truck pulled up to the spot where Hannity was standing, the fake cast and crew watching in amazement as the President jumped off the running board of the truck and walked up to Hannity.

"Thanks for the call, Sean," said the President, shaking his hand.

"Well, I knew you were in New York and would want to know about this," said the beaming FOX anchor, well-aware of how much his act of loyalty to the President would help his brand and ratings.

"You were right. You're a great friend, Sean! Really great!" said an energized President Trump, scanning the area, with his right hand held out to block the lights from the CBS production crew, so he could see better. "Now where's that Nancy Cordes? She's going to get number one on my *Fake News Awards* this year. You hear me, number one!"

In a ritzy high-rise condo in Manhattan, a sleeping Nancy Cordes, shot straight up in her bed screaming, "Nooooooo!!"

Her husband Harald was awoken by the outburst and sat up to see what had happened, "What's wrong, Nancy? What happened?" he asked, still half-asleep.

"I had a terrible dream! I won the Trump *Fake News Awards*! And Sean Hannity and Donald Trump were there, and…oh my, it was the worst moment of my life!"

"That's impossible," said her loving husband, placing his hand on her shoulder. "You could never be accused of Fake News."

Just then, the pink-covered cellphone on the nightstand next to the bed began playing the ringtone from musical artist Rachel Platten's *Fight Song*. Nancy, thinking it was the newsroom, quickly answered. "Hello," she said, with a mixed look of concern and curiosity on her face.

"Hello Nancy, I had a very uneasy feeling a moment ago and it woke me up. Are you having a bad dream or something?" asked the very familiar voice on the other end of the phone.

"My goodness, how did you know?" asked the now smiling and wide-awake CBS national news reporter.

"Well you know, we're that close. There's a bond there, you know. I can feel your pain."

"Well thank you so much for calling, but I'm okay," Cordes said, now beaming.

"Okay, well you call me if I can help. You know how much I appreciate you. You're a great friend. You've always been there for me."

"I appreciate that, but I'm fine. I'll see you soon, Hillary," Cordes said, placing her phone back on the nightstand, now looking oh so happy after a terrible nightmare. She turned to her husband and asked, "So what do we have planned for today?"

He smiled and said, "Oh, I don't know. How about if we go bungee jumping?"

Cordes slapped the palms of her hands against her cheeks and screamed, "Noooo!!!"

CHAPTER 4

TRUMP DELIVERS ON BOLD "FIFTH AVENUE" CAMPAIGN STATEMENT

On a cold and windy Fall Tuesday afternoon in November of 2017, three of the most prominent journalists in the world were seated around the large beautiful mahogany conference room table in the editorial department of the *New York American* newspaper. They were very busy reviewing their investigative reports agenda to determine the priority order of the stories to be pursued. Seated at the table was famed investigative journalist, Richard Koogen; political columnist, Zay Smithers; and managing editor, Albert Dinkins.

On the table for discussion was the fake dossier compiled by former British spy Christopher Steele, hired by Fusion GPS as part of its opposition research for attorney Marc Elias, and then the Democratic Party, in an attempt to sabotage Donald Trump's presidency. The trio of journalists addressed the revelation by Democratic strategist, Donna Brazile, who stated in her book that Hillary Clinton had bought off the financially-strapped Democratic National Committee in order to destroy Senator Bernie Sanders's campaign and win the White House. They moved on to talk about Robert Mueller's on-going investigation into Russia's tampering with the Presidential election and the question about any potential Russian-ties to candidate Donald Trump's campaign.

"Look all three of those stories deserve a great deal of research, but it seems every news organization is pursuing them, wanting to be first," said Dinkins, a very intelligent and distinguished-looking African-American editor who would have the final say about the priority order of the investigative reports. "We need something different, something completely new that no-one else has on their radar."

Richard Koogen, a handsome, middle-aged, veteran reporter, who maintained a slim hip look with a full head of greying black hair combed neatly to the side, interrupted.

"Look, with the Democrats in hot water because of their continued funding of that fake Trump dossier, I think that's the story," Koogen stated in his famously low, gravelly voice, reminiscent of a jazz DJ working a smoke-filled room of *Jack* drinkers in one of the swanky Manhattan Clubs; a place Koogen would feel right at home.

"Yes, we know, Richard," said Smithers, a tall, scholarly-looking writer with a great sense of humor, who also exhibited a thick mane and wry smile. Smithers had achieved prominence as an investigative journalist, working at a local bar set up to expose corruption by city officials who were shaking down small business owners and accepting payoffs to dismiss safety violations. "And I can't disagree with you, except to say that if we really want to pursue the biggest issue of the day as it relates to our own business, then I think we go after Fake News! It's certainly part of that dossier story, as you well know."

"Fake News huh?" said Dinkins, who missed the days when he could depend on the input from his long-departed assistant editor, Eduardo Goldardo, who always seemed to have a clever quip or pun and good perspective that helped the managing editor. "We are going to do a real news story on Fake News, is that right?"

"Exactly," said Smithers.

"And our readers are going to believe that our real news story on Fake News is really real? And not fake?" asked a somewhat confused Dinkins.

"Right again, Albert," Smithers nodded.

"And we aren't publishing it to represent our own interests or our own industry? Is that right?" the editor continued.

"We will research the hell out of it!" said Smithers. "Report the facts. Leave no doubt about who is behind Fake News! When is it real news? Why has so much real news gone away? Why has it been replaced by self-serving, bias news?"

"I kind of like that, Zay," said Koogen, best known at the paper for his love of books, always encouraging anyone who would listen to, 'Read!'"

"Kind of thought you would, Richard," chuckled Smithers, as his attention quickly shifted to the large flat screen TV on the conference room wall with CNN's Wolf Blitzer filling the picture and the words "Breaking News: Shooting?" in large black capital letters at the bottom.

"Hey, look at this," said Smithers, picking up the TV remote to turn up the sound.

"We have breaking news!" reported Blitzer with a large map of New York City appearing behind him. "According to a call we just received here at CNN from a man named John

Barron, President Donald Trump will reportedly be shooting someone on Fifth Avenue here in Manhattan. Now if you can see this intersection right here, where Fifth Avenue intersects with Fifty-Sixth Street, just a few blocks from Trump Tower, we are told that this is where it will take place in the next ten minutes at approximately 5:00 p.m. Eastern Standard Time. Our caller, John Barron, said he was able to arrange a live video feed from the street cameras exclusively for CNN. We are not sure how credible any of this is, especially claiming that he can arrange for a live feed, but in the tradition of CNN, we will follow this news tip to see if there is indeed anything about to happen here. We must warn you that if this is true, if someone is actually going to be shot, this will be violent. If there are any children in the room, you might want to have them leave."

As the three *New York American* journalists watched, the CNN screen was now filled with a live shot of Fifth Avenue, panning across the area showing the Polo Bar, Gucci, and Abercrombie & Fitch, while Blitzer continued to describe what was happening on the street.

"Well here it is," said Blitzer. "Just as our caller John Barron said, a live shot of Fifth Avenue directly from the street camera. I have to say, I'm a bit relieved. I wasn't sure how he was going to pull that off. Now as you can see, there are a good number of people on Fifth Avenue this afternoon, as is usually the case with so many tourists and shoppers."

Koogen moved toward the television and slid his bifocals down from his forehead to get a better look. This was a journalist who knew New York better than any reporter in the city. He prided himself on his ability to write detailed exposés on his investigations into corruption, so he started jotting down notes about the CNN coverage.

The camera shot of Fifth Avenue panned across the pedestrians and stopped on a short man with an average build, wearing black-framed glasses, and dressed in a beige trench coat and fashionable black fedora. The camera shot followed him as he crossed the street, as though someone was directing the shot.

"Now here is a shot of man crossing the street who looks to be carrying a newspaper, which appears to be the *New York American*," said Blitzer, with more than a note of confusion in his voice as he watched the camera shot follow the man across the street. "I had always thought street cameras just provide a wide shot, but apparently this one can pan across crowds and zoom in on individuals. New street-cam technology, I guess. Remember, we were told by John Barron that this is an exclusive to CNN."

Richard Koogen grabbed the TV remote from the conference table, "Excuse me everyone. I would like to check that."

Koogen changed the channel to ABC which was carrying the same exact scene from Fifth Avenue. Flipped to NBC, same scene. CBS, same. FOX News, they had prime time host Sean Hannity on Fifth Avenue, with their own live shot under a FOX News tent, as if they had been planning it for weeks.

"Exclusive huh?" laughed Koogen. "Doesn't anyone at CNN ever monitor the competition?"

Blitzer continued his report with such great enthusiasm that comes with delivering an exclusive that all other news organizations will have to report later, crediting CNN, or so he thought. "The camera is zooming in here and you can now see the face of the man and it appears to be...oh my... it is. That's our CNN boss, Jeff Zucker. Oh no! I hope this is just some sort of crazy coincidence."

Blitzer then looked off camera to his producer and asked, "How does a street camera zoom in on someone and why is it Jeff Zucker? That's awfully strange, don't you think…? No…? Oh…! Okay."

As the three legendary journalists in the conference room at the *New York American* heard Blitzer report that it was Zucker, they all moved toward the television screen to get a good look at the scene being described.

"I hope he's not saying that Zucker is about to get shot, is he?" asked Smithers.

"I hope not," Dinkins blurted back. "I mean if it's true that someone is going to be shot, that's unbelievable! Richard, you need to get down there. And bring Paul Velasquez. We need photos of this."

"We are obviously very concerned and upset by what we have just learned here and are going to take a commercial break," said the famed CNN newsman. After the short commercial break, Blitzer returned, smiling, and with a great deal of renewed energy said, "We are back with this breaking news, exclusive to CNN! No need to check any other channels. We were told we have it exclusively!"

"Oh, they know," said Dinkins. "They are just…well… faking it."

"We received a tip today from a man named John Barron who said that someone was going to be shot on Fifth Avenue in the next ten minutes," continued Blitzer. "Well, the good news is that no one has been shot and we are already past ten minutes since receiving the call, now at 5:02 p.m. Eastern Standard time. Perhaps this is all a hoax, however, if you want to contact any family or friends to let them know about this potentially violent and tragic event to be shown here exclusively on CNN, this would be the time to do it. Remember, we will be showing, exclusively, anything that happens on Fifth Avenue, especially a shooting, if it does occur. And if you miss it for any reason, we will have replays and slow motion of all surrounding violence, adding sound effects for dramatic effect. Because we are CNN, The Most Trusted Name in News!"

Smithers and Dinkins just stood in the conference room gazing wide-eyed at the television, wondering just how desperate CNN had to be to promo a potential tragic incident which seemingly could end up with their boss getting shot.

"This is terrible!" said Smithers, pulling out his cellphone and pressing one of his contact's phone numbers. "Yes honey, turn on CNN. There's a horrific incident being reported. Can you record it? Yes, thanks."

Dinkins turned to the others and said, "I'm appalled by this, just appalled. Please tell everyone in the newsroom to come in here to watch this appalling news coverage. And someone call Jimmy Johns and get some sandwiches in here fast!"

As about a dozen city-side reporters entered the conference room, Wolf Blitzer appeared once again.

"We are back with this breaking news about a tip we received from John Barron saying there would be a shooting on Fifth Avenue here in New York City," said the gray-bearded legendary television anchor. "Now take a look at this. Here is the live feed from Fifth Avenue. For those just tuning in, you should be aware this is not a normal street camera. This camera pans across and zooms in for specific shots. No one here at CNN has ever heard of this new technology, but, given that we are being provided with this as an exclusive from our tipster, a Mr. John Barron, we are quite thankful for this great video coverage."

Once again Blitzer turned toward his producer who was off camera and said, "Has anyone called Zucker to let him know about what is happening here and he may be in danger…? No…? Oh…! Okay."

The *New York American* editorial staff watched this display of lunacy, struggling to believe what they had just heard, as they devoured their Jimmy Johns sandwiches.

"Hey Ginny, call the cops right now," Dinkins said to his administrative assistant. "If they aren't letting Zucker know about the trouble he may be in, then you darn well know they didn't call the cops to report this situation."

"Well, one of the other networks probably alerted the police, right?" said Smithers.

"You really think so, Zay?" asked Dinkins, with a strong tone of sarcasm in his voice.

"You're right," said Smithers. "Ginny better call the cops."

Blitzer was now standing next to the screen pointing at the scene.

"Now the camera seems to be zooming in over the right shoulder of our boss, Jeff Zucker, who is carrying that beautiful red and white CNN umbrella. And it seems to be focusing on that tall, rather large man behind him, who is looking into the window of the restaurant. It looks like he is actually using that window as a mirror to comb his reddish, no, orange hair. Now he is taking off his large tan trench coat, handing it to the man standing next to him. He is stepping onto a scale on the sidewalk outside the restaurant. It looks like one of those scales that measures height and weight. The owner must have put it out there as a gimmick for his customers waiting for a table. Oh wow, look at that! Three hundred, thirty-nine pounds! Now he is lifting the metal rod to check his height… six-foot one-inch…but he's lifting up the rod higher and standing on his tippy toes, six-foot three-inches. Now he is stepping off the scale, putting his trench coat back on and… oh wait! No…it couldn't be! He is turning around and oh my God! Yes, it is President Donald Trump. Ladies and gentlemen, this is unbelievable! The President of the United States is standing on Fifth Avenue where we are told a shooting is about to occur. Wait, you can see there are several Secret Service agents fairly close to him, so that's good."

Blitzer once again turned toward his off-camera producer and asked, "Shouldn't someone call the White House and let them know about this…? No…? Oh…! Okay."

Blitzer turned back toward the viewing audience with somewhat of an embarrassed smile and said, "Oh, here is the President quickly making his way right down the middle of Fifth Avenue, which apparently has been blocked off. It looks like the President is headed toward Jeff Zucker. Mr. Trump is now waving off the four Secret Service agents behind him. He appears to be taking something out of the right pocket of his large trench coat. Oh, and the camera is zooming in again. How about that? Just as if a TV news director were directing this. Oh my! The President has just taken a .357 Magnum handgun out of his coat pocket. That's big! Now he is reaching into the left side of his coat and pulling something out. It looks like a mirror. Apparently he feels it's time to check his hair again. Oh, there goes the zoom again to give us a close-up. You can see that even with a firearm in one hand and Trump-logoed gold mirror in the other, President Trump is continuing to wave off the Secret Service detail and is hurrying toward our leader here at CNN, Jeff Zucker, who is holding that beautiful CNN umbrella in his right hand."

Blitzer quickly turned toward his off-camera producer, "Are you sure someone shouldn't call Zucker…? No…? Oh…! Okay."

Dinkins yelled out to Ginny, "Did you get ahold of the cops about this…? Yes…? Oh…! Okay."

Blitzer was now visibly sweating. "Now it looks like the Secret Service agents are directing a large crowd of people toward Mr. Zucker as well. Trump is closing in on Zucker, who is unaware that the President is following him with a very powerful weapon. The large crowd of 300 to 400 people are being directed by the Secret Service to stand right behind Mr. Trump. That's quite a scene!"

Just then, FOX News host, Sean Hannity wearing a red "Make America Great Again" cap, was seen running into the intersection of Fifty-Sixth and Fifth Avenue with his camera crew, approaching the President and conducting an exclusive live interview.

Blitzer turned to his producer, "I thought this was an exclusive…? No…? Oh…! Okay."

"Apparently he didn't know," said Dinkins.

Hannity finished his interview with President Trump, which the CNN viewers could not hear, meaning many probably bolted CNN for FOX News at that point.

"Trump is now yelling something toward Zucker and if someone could just turn up the street level microphones perhaps we can hear what he is saying," Blitzer reported.

Just then, President Trump's voice was heard yelling, "Zucker, you are a backstabbing traitor! I made you at NBC with *The Apprentice* and now you have gone out of your way at CNN to report Fake News about me all day long. Let me set the record straight. I never had access to those hacked WikiLeaks documents and I never overfed those fish with the Japanese prime minister! I know more about how to feed fish properly than anyone. It's all Fake News! All of it! And you know it! I know it! Because I know more about the news business than anyone! Anyone! You hear me Zucker?"

Smithers turned to Dinkins, "See, Fake News! That's the story."

Dinkins nodded, "Yep."

Trump then turned toward the crowd behind him and said, "That man there is the head of CNN. He is the one responsible for all the Fake News they are reporting about me. Also, this street we are standing on is Fifth Avenue, which is very important information for all of you to know, given one of my very perceptive campaign statements."

Trump then turned back toward Zucker, who was only fifteen feet in front of the wild-eyed Trump, looking directly at him with fear filling his eyes. With his right hand, Trump lifted his Magnum toward Zucker.

"Wait!" shouted Zucker. "Don't!"

"Okay, I won't," said Trump, who then, true to form, opened up with the powerful, shiny hardware. The large crowd behind Trump did not seem to be upset by the sight of Zucker flying backwards and onto the pavement with the color of red splattered all over his coat, fedora, and CNN umbrella.

"Oh no, not the umbrella!" moaned Blitzer.

Many in the crowd had their iPhones out and were taking pictures and recording video of the tragic and disturbing event, while a white blimp flew overhead with three large red letters across it reading *NRA*. One of the four Secret Service agents was reloading for Trump, while another was taking photos with a long-range zoom camera and the other two were filming the moment with a Hollywood-level, state-of-the-art digital camera.

All of a sudden Trump stopped firing, tossed his weapon to the ground and turned toward the large crowd to say, "Now, I have just shot someone on Fifth Avenue. Who would still vote for me?"

Four hundred hands shot straight up in the air simultaneously, as smiles crossed the sea of senior citizens' faces, along with a sprinkling of a few young people, in their 50s, mixed into the crowd.

"That's what I thought," said Trump, as he waved to his adoring fans, then stepped into the back seat of the black Chevy Suburban which had just pulled up to the curb. As the large SUV began driving off, the back window came down and Trump's very large head appeared as he shouted out, "We're making America great again! Also, I just checked my height and weight today. I'm six-foot three-inches, two hundred and thirty-nine pounds. Perfect shape!" Smiling from ear to ear, he gave the crowd his familiar thumbs up sign, closed the window, and drove off into the shadows of the tall skyscrapers lining Fifth Avenue.

Just then, several New York Police squad cars with blaring sirens came flying up Fifth Avenue to the scene of the incident. In only a few minutes, dozens of police swarmed the crime scene with Swat teams, ambulances, and Fire Department trucks pulling up for this major emergency. Richard Koogen was the first newspaper reporter on the scene, but within a few minutes, every television news crew in the city arrived to cover this horrific scene, along with a hoard of newspaper and radio reporters, with digital recorders capturing interviews being conducted with eyewitnesses. A few feet away from the fallen and bloodied Zucker stood Paul Velasquez, the sound of his camera shutter echoing off the Fifth Avenue buildings with each photo taken.

In American history, the only political event that could compare to this moment was when Thomas Jefferson's Vice President Aaron Burr shot and killed former Treasury Secretary Alexander Hamilton in a gentlemen's duel. This was no gentlemen's duel. This was blatant murder in front of hundreds of on-lookers, whom apparently would still vote the murderer back into the White House.

Koogen was somewhat surprised to see just how badly Zucker looked laying on the ground.

"Trump may get the death penalty for this," said a tall young cop standing next to him.

"Only if the judge is a Democrat," Koogen said, only half-jokingly. "I would really want to know if he actually could still win the Presidency having shot someone on Fifth Avenue, just like he said."

"Not a chance," sad the cop, as he looked down at the CNN chief lying in a pool of blood on the red-stained pavement of Fifth Avenue, with dozens of police and medical personnel attending to him. The doctor who had been working so hard to try and revive Zucker, slowly stood up, indicating to all around that there was nothing more he could do for him. The doctor looked around and said very loudly, "There's nothing wrong with this man!"

"What?" said Koogen. "What did he say?"

Just then a familiar large black SUV pulled up to the curb and out jumped a smiling President Donald Trump. At the same time, the seemingly lifeless and bloodied Jeff Zucker jumped up to his feet like an experienced gymnast, then wiped off the fake blood that had been smeared across his face, as Velasquez snapped photos of this now surreal moment.

The crowd looked on aghast, having no understanding of what had just taken place.

President Trump jogged over to Zucker, joined hands with him, faced the crowd, and began taking bows, like two veterans of the theater. "Thank you! Thank you very much! Thank you for coming!" said the smiling President of the

United States, who opened Zucker's jacket to show the crowd the bullet-proof vest he was wearing. "That was fun!"

Then Trump stepped forward to address the crowd.

"Ladies and gentlemen, in association with my good friend, once again, Mr. Jeff Zucker, we have now given you real Fake News! Every news outlet in America and many across the globe have reported that I have killed someone on Fifth Avenue. Well, I didn't kill someone on Fifth Avenue, so it's Fake News! You see Fake News! But the people who said they would vote for me anyway, that was Real News! You see Real News! So, I think I have made my point here, haven't I."

Koogen just shook his head in utter disbelief and raised his hand, "Mr. President, exactly what point have you made here?"

"Well, I think it's very clear to everyone except your news organization at the *New York American*, Mr. Koogen," said Trump. "You see the point is that I'm right. I'm always right. And I always will be right. And when you say I'm wrong, well, you're the one who is wrong and it's Fake News! See. That's the point here."

That evening, news outlets across the nation reported the crazed events that took place on Fifth Avenue that day. Somehow, President Trump had proved his bold campaign statement, while not actually hurting anyone, except of course that beautiful CNN umbrella.

Back in the editorial department of the *New York American*, Dinkins turned to Smithers and said, "You were right. Fake News! That's the story. Let's pursue it first thing Monday morning."

And the two award-winning journalists headed out the door to meet their pals, Koogen and Velasquez, for several beers and many more laughs at their favorite newsman's watering hole, "Citizen Kane's Pub."

CHAPTER 5

THE DONALD'S ENCOUNTER WITH A BLUE FAIRY

Donald J. Trump, the 45th President of the United States, sat at his large Resolute desk in the sunlit Oval Office, reading the *Fact Checker* column in the June 1, 2018, edition of *The Washington Post*, stating that the President had made 3,251 false or misleading statements in his first 497 days in office.

The *Fact Checker* column, written by Glenn Kessler, Salvador Rizzo, and Meg Kelly, became a very popular go-to read for many Americans, presenting daily fact-checking analysis of President Trump's statements. The stories basically indicate that the leader of the free world, the most powerful man on the planet, is no fan of the truth. *The Washington Post* promotes the column as, "Every suspect claim made by President Trump during his presidency in office, in one place."

In the daily stories, the highly-respected newspaper's fact-checkers examine each of President Trump's statements for accuracy, based purely on the actual facts, not commentary or speculation. When wrong, the *Post* assigns a Pinocchio rating of one to four, based on the severity of the misinformation.

Pinocchio is the character created in the 1883 novel by author Carlo Collodi, and later recreated in the 1940 Walt Disney animated film. For the fact-checking stories, Pinocchio is deemed the appropriate term, because the character is best known for his nose growing every time he tells a lie. And with each continuing lie, his nose grows longer and longer, so he can't lie without those around him knowing that he is fibbing. In the President's case, he can't lie either, because *The Washington Post* acts as his growing nose; the coverage of his lies getting longer and longer, so those around the world know when he is fibbing.

"How dare they!" belted out an angry President Trump, slamming the newspaper down on his desk. "How dare they publish those lies in *The Washington Post*? The failing *Washington Post*!"

He shifted his large brown-leather executive chair toward the phone on the left corner of his desk and pressed the intercom button, "Madeleine, get Huckleberry Finn in here, would you?"

"Yes sir, Mr. President," said Madeleine Westerhout, the twenty-six-year-old administrative assistant, who knew he was referring to Sarah Huckabee Sanders. Within minutes, the White House Press Secretary entered the Oval Office, carrying a clipboard and a stack of *Washington Post* newspapers.

"Have you seen this *Washington Post* story on me, claiming I have made 3,251 false statements to the public since I took office?" groaned the President, his face turning from bright orange to bright red.

"Yes, President Trump, and we had our fact-checkers double-check their fact-checkers and I can tell you with absolute certainty, that the *Post* is wrong!" said Huckabee Sanders, looking down and to the right, organizing her papers, avoiding eye contact with the President.

"They have it wrong! I knew it!" said a now delighted Donald Trump. "Fact-checking the fact-checkers, I like that! Good media management there, Huckleberry. Remind me later to give you a raise, a big one."

"Thank you, President Trump, I will do that," she said, continuing to look down, shuffling the papers as she spoke.

"So, of the 3,251 statements I made that they claim are false, how many were accurate?"

"Well, we know that not all of them were false," she informed her smiling boss.

"Beautiful, that's what I wanted to hear," he said, tossing his newspaper into the empty waste basket. "Garbage, pure garbage! So how many were accurate though?"

"Well, we don't like to get into the specific numbers...."

"How many?"

"One!"

"One? That's all, just one?" he said standing up quickly, angrily slamming his hand down on the desk, appalled that there weren't at least two.

"Just one, but it's an important one," she explained.

"Oh! Which one? Which statement did I make that was accurate?" he asked, looking slightly calmer.

"It was last week at your big event in Nashville," she continued.

"Ah yes, Nashville," the President said, tilting his head back, recalling the wonderful rally where he spoke to 5,500 enthusiastic, cheering Trumpsters.

"It was when you said, and I quote, 'What do I look like: a moron?'"

Trump quickly snapped out of his nostalgic Nashville moment. "Wait, I had that right?"

"You did, at least according to Rex Tillerson, Steve Bannon, and pretty much everyone else who has ever worked for you. We fact-checked it."

"Even you, Huckleberry?"

"No, no, not me, Mr. President, I would never...."

"That's good to know."

"So perhaps this is a good time to remind you about that big raise you promised," she said, now looking directly at him.

Just then, the intercom buzzed. "Yes, Madeleine," said the President, pressing the intercom button on his internal White House phone.

"Your guest has arrived, President Trump," said the energetic young brunette, who began working for candidate Trump in 2016, but became his administrative assistant in June of 2017, and is considered highly dependable. "Should I show him in?"

"Yes, please, and have some sweet tea sent in," said the President, taking the stack of *Washington Post* newspapers from Sanders and tossing them into the waste basket. "I believe he will enjoy that."

"Yes, Mr. President, I agree," she said, as the President escorted her to the door.

"Huckleberry, thank you very much for your report. I'm now going to be conducting a private meeting with an expert on this subject and will call you later to discuss it," he informed her.

"Yes, President Trump," said Sanders, who nearly bumped into Ms. Westerhout, entering the bright white wooden door with a young man right behind her, who looked to be about twelve or thirteen years old. A puzzled look crossed Sanders's face, as she wondered why the President would call in a boy to address *The Washington Post Fact Checker* issue. Ms. Westerhout led the boy into the office, skipping an introduction, then quickly ducked back out to ensure the drinks were on the way.

"Hello President Trump," said the young man, politely reaching up to shake hands with his very tall host, who was at least two feet taller than him.

"Hello, I'm so glad you were able to make it in from Italy on such short notice," said Mr. Trump, escorting him over to the plush, floral-patterned, cream-colored sofa where he was looking forward to having a great discussion. "I'm so glad to have finally met you. I know you will be able to give me some insight that will help my presidency, my administration, and quite frankly, the world."

"Thank you, Mr. President. I will do my best," said the boy, who was dressed in a bright yellow shirt with a black vest and blue bow tie, knee-length red shorts held up by suspenders, matching red shoes, white gloves, and a yellow wool hat with a red feather jutting out from a blue band that encircled it.

"Well, as you may have heard, Pinocchio, since I've run for office, your name keeps coming up, as the Fake News media keeps claiming that I'm not telling the truth," said Trump, who sat in the elegant high-backed citrine yellow armchair, closest to the boy.

"Oh, I don't like to hear that, Mr. President," said the wide-eyed Pinocchio, sitting back on the sofa, nervously clicking his shoes together. "They used to tell me I was lying all the time as well, you know."

"Exactly, I mean, as I have said to so many people in the past, I don't lie!" Trump insisted. "I'm not a liar. I just position my information a little differently. Is it my fault that I'm like, really smart, a genius quite frankly, and some aren't able to comprehend what I am saying?"

"Position?" asked the boy.

"Yes, you know, position the information, so it may seem a little complicated for some, especially for the mainstream media who believe it's misleading, non-factual, fabricated, made up, false," the President explained, gesturing with his hands to emphasize each point.

"You mean lies?" asked the very trusting young boy.

"Well, no, because I don't lie, so...."

"So, can they tell when you are ly...not telling the tr... positioning the information?"

"Well they like to fact-check everything I say and that seems to be the main problem here," said Trump. "And quite frankly, that's why I invited you in for a meeting today."

"Checking facts is a good idea...."

"No, no, it's not," Trump interrupted. "It's really not, because they do an analysis of my statements, then check them against the facts, assigning a Pinocchio rating based on how badly they believe I am lying. You see?"

"Yes, I think so."

"So when they believe there is some shading of the facts, I get one Pinocchio; when they say there have been significant exaggerations, I get two Pinocchios; significant factual errors or contradictions, three Pinocchios; and four Pinocchios is for the whoppers."

"Burger King?"

"No, lies! Big ones!"

"Oh, I see, they're using my name because I'm famous for my nose growing whenever I lie. Is that it?" asked Pinocchio.

"Exactly, and let me tell you, young man, according to the *Post*, I've been living in Whopperville since I started my campaign," Trump said, shaking his head in disgust. "It's disgraceful! A complete disgrace!"

"Oh, I'm sorry to hear that, Mr. President," Pinocchio said, fully able to relate to that type of criticism.

"Well thank you, but I'm hoping you can tell me how I can avoid these accusations about lying? I mean, you're a real boy now, so you're in the clear, right?"

The young man jumped up off the sofa and put his hands behind his back as he strode around the Oval Office in deep thought, considering President Trump's dilemma and how he might be able to help him.

"Well, you see, President Trump, the man who made me was Geppetto," Pinocchio explained about the woodcarver.

"And the man who made me was ruthless Roy Cohn," President Trump explained about the bully lawyer, his mentor.

"But I was just a wooden marionette and Geppetto wanted me to become a real boy, which was just a wish upon a star, until the Blue Fairy showed up and brought me to life," said the pacing boy, stopping to look at the President.

"Blue Fairy. You mean a Democrat?" asked Trump.

"No, an actual Blue Fairy. You know, a beautiful lady with a pretty face, golden hair, dressed in a long, blue, sparkling gown with light blue wings, holding a magic wand with a star on the end," explained the four-foot-tall boy.

"Sounds like a lady I met in Russia once," said Trump. "And I was the star at the end of the wand she was holding, if you know what I mean."

"She was wonderful!" Pinocchio continued, ignoring the President's comment. "And she put Jiminy Cricket in charge of guiding my conscience so I would do the right thing."

"Oh I see, that's what I was hoping General Kelly would do for me, but I'm not so sure that's working out," the President said, slowly shaking his head back and forth.

"Oh my, doesn't he try to lead you in the right direction? Do the right thing?" asked the brightly-dressed boy, still pacing the room with hands clasped behind his back.

"Well sure, but I'm not listening to that BS. I mean, I'm my own best advisor. I'm going to do what I want to do, no matter what anyone tells me, except for me of course. I'll listen to me. I'm good that way," said Trump, who stood to greet a tall, slim, Irish-looking White House staff waiter who entered the Oval Office, carrying a round tray with a pitcher of icy sweet tea and two glasses. "Oh thank you, Shamus. Pinocchio, I thought I would have sweet tea brought in. Do you like sweet tea?"

The young boy watched Shamus pour the delicious-looking light brown chilled tea into each glass, and said, "Oh I love sweet tea. It's my favorite."

His nose began to grow.

"I mean, I drink it all the time," he said, noticing his nose growing even more. "What I meant to say was that…well, the truth is that lemonade is my favorite, but I like sweet tea just fine."

His nose reduced back to its normal size as Shamus exited the room and President Trump sat in his armchair, sipping his glass of sweet tea.

"Oh, so I see," said the President, who couldn't help but notice Pinocchio's nose-growing exhibition. "So apparently, you still have that nose thing going on, eh?"

"Well, even though I'm a real boy, the Blue Fairy told me she is still going to have it grow when I lie as a reminder."

"That damn Blue Fairy again. Any chance her name is Hillary?"

A blank look filled Pinocchio's face. "No, I just call her Blue Fairy."

"Well I just call her Crooked Hillary," said Trump laughing, and slapping his knee. "I love that name. It's one of my favorites."

Pinocchio stopped pacing and looked over at the President, having no idea why he was laughing.

"But seriously Pinocchio, where did you go wrong and how did you solve it?" asked the President, watching the young man intently, hoping he could solve a major problem for him.

The boy began pacing around the room once again, hands clasped behind his back, thoughtfully considering the question, "Well, when John the Fox and Gideon the Cat convinced me to join Stromboli's puppet show, and I became a big star, my ego went wild, and I thought I could do anything."

"I know what you mean," said President Trump. "That's pretty much how I felt after I became a big star with my own show, *The Apprentice*. Plus, I got to fire everybody, which I really enjoyed. So it was a win-win for me."

"And then I ended up on Pleasure Island," Pinocchio continued.

"Oh, Pleasure Island, I've been there," said a smiling Donald Trump. "Many times! Many, many times! Cost me a bit of dough though. Had to pay off the gals to keep their lips sealed, shut their yaps, hit their internal mute button. Well, actually I didn't pay them. My lawyer did, Michael Cohen. He's good at that kind of thing. Got to have an intermediary, Pinocchio. Someone to take the heat, if the ladies don't stick to the deal, you know."

"No I don't, but I had this really bad kid, Lampwick, who was getting me into trouble all the time!" said the boy.

"Lampwick? Any relation to a fellow named Steve Bannon?" asked Trump.

"Is Steve Bannon loud and crazy with wild hair and makes you do all the wrong things?"

"That's the guy!" shouted Trump, startling the young boy so much that he fell to the floor. "How did you get away from him?"

The boy smiled, "The Blue Fairy told me that I could become a real boy if I prove myself to be brave, truthful, and unselfish."

"Brave, truthful, and unselfish," said a puzzled-looking Trump. "Isn't there another way?"

"No, that was it. I had to straighten up and do the right thing. Stop lying!"

"Yeah, I see. You're not leaving me a lot of options here," said the President, standing, clasping his hands behind his back, and pacing the floor, thoughtfully considering the situation. "So you're saying, if I stop ly…positioning the information, then this whole Pinocchio thing will go away?"

"It worked for me!" said Pinocchio with a big smile, feeling as though they had found a path for President Trump to be brave, truthful, and unselfish, so he could become a real man.

❧

Two days later, Sarah Huckabee Sanders entered the Oval Office once again, this time holding a notepad and pen, speaking directly to the President who was seated behind his desk. "Yes, Mr. President, you wanted to see me about that raise."

"What? I never promised you a raise!" said the President.

"Well, that's a whopper," muttered Sanders to herself, looking down to the right, shuffling the papers in her notepad.

"No, I wanted to update you about my meeting with my *Fact Checker* expert," the President informed her.

"You mean, Pinocchio?" Sanders asked, raising her eyebrows, wondering what great knowledge could have possibly come from that strange encounter.

"Yes, he's a great young man, the best! Really helped me. Pointed me in the right direction. One of the things he convinced me about was replacing General Kelly."

"You're kidding?"

"No, I'm quite serious. That four-foot boy in the brightly-colored costume who used to be a wooden marionette talked some real sense into me," said Trump.

"But who will replace General Kelly?" asked Sanders.

"That's a good question, Huckleberry," he said with a look of hope in his eyes. "That's why I looked out of my Oval Office window toward the sky two nights ago and I wished upon a star for the right person to guide me down the right path. Then I clicked my heels together three times and said there's no place like home, the White House, and lo and behold, I found him."

Just then, the President began to break into song, "When you wish upon a…."

The intercom buzzed, forcing Trump to stop singing.

"Thank God for that intercom!" said Sanders, as Trump pressed the intercom button on his phone.

"Yes, Madeleine," he said.

"Mr. President, your next appointment is here," said Ms. Westerhout.

"Very good. Send him right in," said Trump, standing and walking toward the door to greet his guest. "Huckleberry, I'd like you to meet this fellow. He will become my new Chief of Staff. Very impressive guy! The best!"

And through the door, Madeleine Westerhout entered with a very short, strange looking guest, dressed in blue top hat, black tail coat, red vest, brown pants, and blue shoes, and carrying a red umbrella.

"Mr. President," said his administrative assistant. "Please allow me to introduce you to Mr. Jiminy Cricket."

CHAPTER 6

OPRAH'S DECISION ON RUNNING FOR PRESIDENT

For years, the world-famous Oprah Winfrey, beloved talk show host to millions of women across America, has been asked if she would ever run for President of the United States. Her answer has always been the same, "No!" However, her speech at the Golden Globes held at the Beverly Hilton Hotel on January 7, 2018, acknowledged that the day had come when women no longer had to endure assault and abuse by evil men. She said the time had come when women could now step forward against that abuse and that "a new day is on the horizon."

The reaction to her talk was overwhelmingly positive across the entire media spectrum, with many news commentators calling on Oprah to run for President in 2020. Her fans were extremely excited, making their appeals to her via social media, saying, "We need you Oprah! You have to save our country! You have to save us from that arrogant, foul-mouthed, misogynist, greedy pig in the White House."

In the days after her talk, friends and those who know Oprah best shared their opinion on this issue, most saying that they didn't believe she would run. Oprah had been walking somewhat of a fine line, saying she was "intrigued by the idea," leading many of her supporters to believe that she might actually run. She heard the many voices and the extensive news coverage and Oprah, being human, seemed to be affected by these calls for her to run for the most important office in the land.

When she went home from the Hollywood awards ceremony that evening, she spoke with her very close friend, Gayle King, who Oprah had included in her speech saying, "Gayle is the definition of what a friend is." All of the specifics of their discussion were kept completely private, completely confidential, never to be made public, until King revealed them the next day on *CBS This Morning*.

"Oprah and I talked about it late into the night," King told Norah O'Donnell and the CBS viewers. "And I don't think she will run, although she is intrigued by the idea."

Oprah's longtime boyfriend, Stedman Graham, had been asked by a reporter from the *L.A. Times* about Oprah running and said, "She would do it, but it is ultimately up to the people."

Despite the statement from King, which was viewed as "the Gospel from Oprah," the media at large wasn't accepting the vagueness of the answer and kept pushing to find out if she might actually run. After a few weeks of dominating the news cycle, the Queen of Talk had some time to really consider what a run for the White House would mean for her, and granted an exclusive interview to a reporter whom she trusted.

The powerful *Chicago Times* media reporter Bobby Reeder is the journalist who helped Oprah achieve her initial stardom, writing about her talent and audience appeal quite often when she was the host of the local morning television show, *AM Chicago*. Reeder was granted the exclusive interview with the understanding that Oprah would also have the discussion recorded by one of her television crews for historical purposes. The media expert suspected that she made the request so she could provide the recording to one of the national television networks as a broadcast exclusive. And there was no doubt in Reeder's mind which network, and which program, would receive it. But, to get the interview, he agreed to it.

Reeder was an old-school, traditional reporter, who knew he wanted to be a journalist from an early age and practiced writing reports as a child. His mentor at the *Chicago Times*, the ultra-talented Daniel Ruth, set the standard in journalism for him. He told Bobby on his first day at the paper, "Get all the facts, get two solid sources, and don't be influenced by anyone trying to sway the story in the direction of their own opinion or agenda. And that includes your associates in the newsroom!"

Oprah knew if she granted the interview to one of the top media reporters in the country, Reeder, who was so well known for his journalistic integrity, her comments would be taken seriously and every other newspaper, TV news outlet, and radio station in the world would report on the interview. So, she was going to give him the straight story.

"I am going to speak the truth, the most powerful tool we have," she told King and Graham about her intent for the interview.

So, on Wednesday, January 24, with the sky blue and sun shining bright, Reeder drove up to Oprah's twenty-eight million dollar, forty-five-acre estate in Montecito, California. He checked in at the gated entrance where a very tall, athletic-looking African-American security guard in bullet-proof vest stepped out of the guard-shack and approached the reporter's

2004 silver Pontiac G-6 Sedan. The guard seemed to recognize the car immediately and as Reeder opened the window, he asked him, "Were you one of the winners of the…."

"No!" Reeder cut him off, knowing where the question was going. "I actually bought it off of one of the winners, who advertised it on the web."

"Found out about the taxes, eh?" said the security guard.

"Yep," said Reeder.

"Well, they still won a free car, right?" said the guard. "May I see your ID?"

The greying, bookish-looking, sixty-one-year-old media reporter showed the smiling guard his license and reporter's badge and drove through the now opened, iron-cast, spiked gate. Within a few minutes, Reeder was entering Oprah's very well-decorated Hollywood home and was escorted by an Irish maid, Bridgette, to the back, where Oprah was sitting poolside reading a book on which Reeder could see the title, *What I Know For Sure* by Oprah Winfrey.

"Ms. Winfrey," said Bridgette in a gentle tone. "Mr. Reeder is here for the interview."

Oprah didn't look up immediately but finished reading a sentence in the book, then laughed loudly, closed the book, and said out loud, "I have to agree with myself on this. I just knew it. And I knew that I knew it, ya know."

"Hello Oprah," said Reeder, extending his right hand to shake with the legendary woman known in every corner of the world.

"Oh, hello Bobby," said Oprah, struggling for a moment to get up from the very comfortable lounge chair. "Really appreciate you flying in from Chicago for this interview."

"No problem there, Oprah," laughed Reeder. "Glad to be in this beautiful weather."

After she offered Reeder something to drink and the Irish maid brought out a beautiful large glass pitcher of iced tea, the reporter and legend walked over to sit on colorful, foam-backed deck chairs, where a production crew was standing ready to record the interview.

"Bobby, would you like my makeup person to touch you up a bit before we get started?" asked Oprah, nodding to a very fashionably-dressed young lady, who was dabbing on cover-up and powder before Reeder could refuse. Within just a few minutes, Reeder was camera-ready and the interview began.

"So, Oprah, as you know," began Reeder in a gentle tone as he adjusted his thick, dark-rimmed glasses. "The entire world, it seems, is now talking about your speech at the Golden Globes and the possibility of you running for President of the United States in 2020 against Donald Trump. Now that you have had some time to really consider it, have you come to a decision?"

Oprah lifted her right hand and placed her index finger against her chin, giving great thought to the question, which was certainly the most obvious question Reeder would be asking that afternoon.

"Yes, Bobby, I have given this some thought," she said, lifting her chin and changing her vocal pattern into that now very familiar sophisticated tone of voice. "I know for certain that many Americans would like me to run for President. I have heard it and read it. It's seems many have become quite obsessed with the idea, which is very flattering. They say that they want me to save the country. They are upset with the current administration and looking for an answer. I get it."

"Do you believe you can save the country?" asked Reeder, feeding her a line that he knew could result in a sensational quote.

"I believe I can do what I can do," said Winfrey, very nicely side-stepping the 'gotcha' question. "The question is, should I run for President, or should I continue my mission to make my contribution through my television network, magazine, and movies? But, I am intrigued by the idea of running for President."

"So you are not going to run?" Reeder asked.

"I didn't say that," Oprah quickly responded. "I have asked God for a sign that I wouldn't miss, and so far, nothing. But, I think if the call from the people becomes loud enough and strong enough, perhaps that would be the sign, and I may have to seriously consider running for President."

Bridgette returned holding a house phone and said, "Ms. Winfrey, I am sorry to interrupt, but we have an urgent call. Mayor Bill De Blasio's office is calling to let us know that 10,000 women have lined up across the George Washington Bridge in New York holding up signs saying, *Oprah Please Run!* They want to know if this will inspire you to run?"

"Let them know I appreciate their efforts and find it intriguing, but at this time, I am not prepared to announce that I am running," Oprah said, looking delighted about the sign of encouragement.

Bridgette walked away, repeating Oprah's response.

"So you don't view that as a sign?" asked Reeder.

"It's a sign, but I'm really looking for a sign with some lightning and thunder attached to it," she said. "You know, stuff that there's no question it's coming from the Almighty."

"So you're not going to run?"

"As I stated to Mayor De Blasio's office. I'm not ready to make any announcement at this time."

"Yes, I see," Reeder continued, looking at his notes. "But that's the question here, because if you do decide to run, like every other politician who has run for President, your professional and personal life will be scrutinized to the greatest degree. Your opponents will dig up every piece of dirt on you, find anyone who has worked for you, or known you, and has bad things to say about you. It's a public undressing every time, and the politicians who somehow survive it usually win. What are your thoughts on trying to survive that ordeal?"

"Well, I have been an open book, so I don't really know what types of things they could say about me that would damage my reputation or image," said Oprah, lifting her chin high, going back to her sophisticated voice.

"Well for starters, your relationship with Gayle King and your supposed relationship with Stedman Graham, your boyfriend or partner," Reeder stated quite directly. "It's all very vague and there have been stories and speculation about it for more than two decades, including the statements made by your former step-mother, Barbara Winfrey."

"Gayle is just my dearest and closest friend in the world," said Oprah. "I said that at the Golden Globes. I hope you aren't suggesting that is Fake News and Stedman is my fake boyfriend. I hope that's not what you are trying to say here Mr. Reeder."

"I'm not saying any such thing Oprah. However, I can guarantee you that within a week of your announcement to run, the truth of your relationship with Gayle King and Stedman Graham, whatever it is, will be published by some conservative news outlet," Reeder said, leaning in to the great lady and looking her directly in the eye, so she understood the magnitude of the decision. "Then, the mass media will be forced to consider publishing that news. All will wait, but one legitimate TV news outlet or newspaper will decide that they need to publish that report. And when they do, the floodgates will open and everyone will report it, even *CBS This Morning*."

"I don't know what you're referring to Bobby," said Oprah, now looking a bit upset.

"Okay, well, aside from that, what about another scandalous incident the GOP will most certainly dig up? There's no doubt that they will go after the day on your talk show when you claimed to have given away a free, brand new twenty-eight-thousand-dollar Pontiac G-6 sedan; a gift, to two hundred and seventy-six of your audience members," said Reeder.

"I did give them a free car and it's one of my favorite moments," said Oprah, her pride from that day on full display.

"Were the cars a gift?" asked Reeder.

"Well, I...." stammered Oprah.

"Who was really the one giving away free cars?"

"Pontiac!"

"And it wasn't charity? It was advertising for them, right?" Reeder pushed.

"Well, yes, instead of buying commercial time on our show, they gave away free cars which turned out to be the best advertisement they ever invested in."

"Yes, but then the audience members found out they had to pay seven thousand dollars in taxes, because it wasn't a gift."

"It was a promotion. A free car! They got a free car!"

"But who got credit for giving away all those free cars?"

"Well, I...I...."

"You did! And you don't think that's going to be resurrected by your opponents who will call it the biggest misrepresentation of charity in the history of television talk shows?"

"I think it was a very nice thing. They didn't have to take the car."

Bridgette entered again holding the phone, "Ms. Winfrey, Donald Trump's office is on the line and would like to know if you will include his new book in the Oprah Book Club."

"What? What book?" asked Oprah.

"Well, they said it has your name in the title, so they thought you might want to put it in your book club."

"Well, what's the title?" she asked, and Bridgette relayed the question over the phone, then replied, "It's titled, *Oprah, I Used to Like You, but Now I Hate You.*"

Oprah just laughed, "Bridgette, please thank Mr. Trump's office, but that won't fit in with our positive mission for the book club."

Bridgette walked out of the room repeating the message over the phone. Reeder just watched this craziness and asked, "Is your life always like this?"

"Every day, Bobby. Every day."

"I'm sorry," he said, now getting a birds-eye view of the life of a mega-celebrity. "Well, I don't want to take up too much more of your time, but your opponents will also try to find former disgruntled employees who worked for you over the years."

"Every employer has disgruntled employees," she responded. "I tried very hard to be very fair to my employees, but there's no question that you can't please everyone."

"That's true, but here's the point," said Reeder, hoping to get a good quote pertaining to Oprah's consideration of entering the political arena. "If you run for President, you will have to get down in the mud with the other politicians, defending everything you have ever done in your life, just so you can win. Then, if you do win, you'll have to get right back down in the mud to fight for every piece of legislation you want to pass. They'll attack your viewpoints! They'll attack you personally! They'll attack everything they can about you, to tear you down, and win whatever battle is being fought at any given time. You will be attacked on social media. That's politics! And I go back to my original question, are you sure you would consider running for President of the United States?"

❧

Three years later, on a cold January 20 in 2021, thousands of supporters were packed in front of the U.S. Capitol Building, where the new President of the United States would be sworn into office on this very historical Inauguration Day. As all of the dignitaries were led to their assigned seats, all eyes were on the doorway, where each was introduced and escorted through the tall, red velvet-tapered doorway and down the royal-blue-rugged steps. Seated in the VIP section, just above where the new President would be sworn in, were Gayle King, Stedman Graham, and Oprah Winfrey, who was working on a new movie based on the true story of a famous woman's decision not to run for President of the United States. In the media section sat Bobby Reeder, whose exclusive story on Oprah Winfrey's decision not to run was published in the Sunday, January 28, 2018 edition of the *Chicago Times* and won him several industry awards, making him one of the most sought-after guests for the cable news talk shows.

When the introduction was made for President Donald Trump and Vice President Michael Pence, the Marine Corps band began playing 'Hail to the Chief.' A loud cackle was heard coming from the front row where each of the former Presidents were seated.

"Ah, hah, hah! Hail to the Chief! How about Goodbye to the Grief!" belted out Hillary Clinton, standing next to her husband, former President Bill Clinton. "*Hit the Road, Jack!* is a more appropriate song for you!" she yelled out, cupping her hands over her mouth to make sure he could hear her as she sang out, "Hit the road, The Donald! Don't you come back no more!"

Trump just looked at her with his now-famous frozen smile. Then, in his usual Presidential style, raised his left arm toward her and flipped her off. The only thing separating him from the Clintons was former Presidents Barack Obama and George W. Bush, who realized they may be called into action if this exchange continued. Obama looked over at former President Clinton and realized he would be of no assistance, since he was too busy hitting on Melania Trump. As Trump sat down, he continued holding up his left middle finger toward Clinton, who responded, "That's right Donald! One finger for one term. That's all you got! Hah!"

"At least I had a term," Trump fired back. "You two-time loser!"

All of the network cameras pulled in for a close-up of the outgoing President, seated just to the left of the podium with his famous golden comb-over being blown by twenty-five-mile-an-hour winds, but not disrupted as the three cans of Gorilla Glue Hairspray were keeping the fake locks in place. Seated next to the outgoing President was his new gold digger wife, Stormy Daniels, who was seated next to Trump's previous gold digger wife, Melania, who had provided the Republican leaders with inside information about her husband that led him not to seek a second term. But it did lead him to seek a divorce and Melania received a settlement of fifty-five million dollars and the Trump Tower in Chicago, where The Donald was never welcome anyway. The inside information she had on video would be far more damaging to Trump than the scandalous stories fabricated in Michael Wolff's book. She was an eye-witness to Trump behind the scenes, with hours of video she had secretly taken on her iPhone, which she described as a lot more incriminating than Wolff's account of an obese seventy-one-year-old man sitting on his bed at night eating cheeseburgers.

Melania said she would use the settlement to fund a training center for former models seeking to marry rich, egotistical, sexually-offensive bastards, then take them for half their net worth and start their own training center. Moments before, when Melania had been introduced and led down the royal-blue steps by a U.S. Marine, both Democrats and Republicans stood to applaud her, including each of the former living Presidents and their wives. The loudest cheers came from Hillary Clinton, who just four years earlier had to endure watching Donald Trump be sworn in only a few feet away from her on the day that she was certain she would be sworn in as the first woman President of the United States.

As former President Clinton greeted Melania, then groped his way past her toward Stormy Daniels, the strong-voiced U.S. Capitol announcer began his next introduction as two U.S. Marines opened the doors, "Ladies and gentlemen, the President-Elect of the United States, Peyton W. Manning!" Loud, boisterous cheers exploded across the nation, America so happy to be greeting a new President, a man they loved, who they knew would lead them back in the right moral direction.

The smiling six-foot five-inch ex-NFL quarterback, ran as an independent and won in a landslide over the Republican candidate, Mike Pence, and the Democratic opponent, Charles Barkley, who felt he lost the election because he couldn't correctly pronounce the word 'ridiculous.' Manning descended down the royal-blue steps, shaking hands with those on both sides of the aisle. The cheers became louder for the man who had won the country over with his refreshingly honest statements and campaign promises, his strong family values, great sense of humor, and commitment to never, ever, deflate the office of the President of the United States.

And from above, a smiling Oprah Winfrey looked down and applauded her approval.

CHAPTER 7

THOUSANDS OF TRUMP SUPPORTERS PROTEST PRESIDENT'S HARMFUL WORDS

Looking out of the window in the Oval Office of the White House, Press Secretary Sarah Huckabee Sanders was very surprised to see a very large group of protestors outside of the tall, spiked iron fence separating the country's most famous residence from the outside world. She had certainly witnessed plenty of protests taking place outside of that tall black fence with groups protesting against President Trump's immigration policies, travel ban, climate change, and always the continual chant to "Resist, Resist, Resist!" Anything Donald Trump proposed usually resulted in an organized protest.

But this protest was very different. The protestors were wearing the familiar red caps with white letters across the front saying, "Make America Great Again." They were holding up signs stating, "Stop the change!" "Don't go back on your word!"

Sanders looked out at this group, feeling a bit confused to say the least, then turned to President Trump who was sitting at his desk watching CNN, MSNBC, and FOX News on the three televisions he had placed on the wall closest to his desk.

"President Trump," she began, sounding more than a bit concerned. "You need to see this protest out here."

"Protest!" Trump smirked, waving her off with his right hand, which was holding the Trump-logoed channel controller. "Huckleberry, there's a protest nearly every day. What do I care? I got my loyal base of supporters, everyone else can move to one of those shithole countries in Africa or Haiti."

"Yes, I know sir," Sanders continued. "But I think this is your base out there protesting. They are wearing the red 'Make America Great Again' caps."

Trump sprang out of his brown-leather Presidential chair so quickly that it sounded like a very loud flatulation. "Excuse me!" he said, which sounded like the first time he was apologetic about anything he had done in his life.

"Oh, that's okay Mr. President," said Sanders, trying not to embarrass her boss about his very loud explosion, which shook some of the photos hanging in the Oval Office.

"Well, it's really not okay, Huckleberry," he said, looking directly at her. "I wish you could control yourself a little better, especially when you're in the White House, the pure house, the house where no intestinal gas should be expelled from the derriere. Are we clear?"

"Yes, of course Mr. President," she said, taking the blame. "I'll load up on the Gas-X so it never happens again."

"I wish you would," said the President, who walked toward the window to see what all the commotion was outside the fence. "Fake! Those are all fake protestors. They're wearing the red caps to try and make the media believe that my base has turned on me. Never!"

Sanders stood next to the President as they watched television news crews walk into the crowd of protestors to get interviews. They could see Major Garrett from CBS, John Roberts from FOX, ABC's Jonathan Karl, and NBC's Peter Alexander.

"Hey, I don't see Jim Acosta," said Sanders, wondering why CNN's White House correspondent wasn't covering this protest. "Oh wait, there he is. Looks like he must have gotten into a shoving match with *The Times*'s Mark Landler and lost. Hah! Love when print and TV reporters get into it. They actually hate each other, but the public doesn't know it."

"Well, I'll have to tweet that out, Huckleberry," laughed Trump. "That's some real news they should know about."

Just then, one of the television screens blared their breaking news music, which caught President Trump's attention as he turned to see:

ABC News

Breaking News: Major Protest at the White House

"Here we go, Huckleberry," said Trump, turning up the volume for the ABC report, loud enough so Sanders wouldn't hear his series of gaseous explosions, which sounded like rapid cannon fire reminiscent of the *1812 Overture*. "Now we will find out what's going on out there."

Sanders had fallen to the floor for a moment, feeling quite dizzy, overcome by the overwhelming stench that now filled the Oval Office.

"Huckleberry, you really have to get that Gas-X," warned the President. "I can't have anyone stinking up this honorable office."

Back outside the White House fence, Karl stood next to a very angry man and asked, "Sir, what is your name and where are you from?"

The very tall, long-haired, stubble-faced, wild-eyed man looked down toward the ABC camera and said, "Tony Pateki from Nashville, Tennessee, and I don't watch ABC!"

"Nice to know that, Mr. Pateki," continued the short, brown-haired, well-dressed reporter, looking up at the man who was nearly a foot taller than him. "We are wondering what sparked this massive protest here today. It's unusual to see so many people wearing the 'Make America Great Again' caps but protesting the President. Can you tell us what this is all about?"

Pateki glared down at ABC's White House correspondent and said in a very angry tone, "He can't do this! President Donald Trump cannot do this to us! We are his loyal followers! This is just plain wrong!"

The puzzled look on Karl's face grew as he held his microphone up to the angry middle-aged man, wearing a red flannel work-shirt and green khaki pants and asked, "What sir? What is wrong? Do you mean the way the President has conducted himself since he got into office? Or perhaps his very mean-spirited immigration policy? Or is this about his racist travel ban? Is that what you mean?"

"No, no, no! Those are all great. We love those policies!" said Pateki with true determination in his eyes. "We are here to protest a very, very important issue. Very important!"

"And what would that be?" asked Karl, now more curious than ever.

"The President can't call Senator Chuck Schumer 'Fake Tears Chuck' last year and then all of a sudden change it to 'Cryin' Chuck' during the budget battle," demanded Pateki.

"What!" yelped Karl, adjusting his brown-framed glasses to get a better look at this crazy man.

"He can't do it! Can't happen! Won't accept it," said the tall man from Nashville. "When he calls him Fake Tears Chuck, he has to stick with Fake Tears Chuck. We are counting on him to maintain his integrity on his hurtful name-calling."

"You're kidding, right?" asked Karl, really confused by thousands of people who would travel to Washington to make this protest.

"Do you know how many T-shirts and caps we printed up with 'Fake Tears Chuck?' Do you know what we paid for design and printing? For storage? This is an outrage!"

Well that explained it to Karl. It was about money.

"So you're saying that you are upset because he changed the name he called Senator Chuck Schumer. Is that right?"

"Damn straight."

Karl turned to the crowd many of whom had been listening to the interview. "Is that why all of you are out here protesting?"

A loud shout went up, "Yes, stop the name change!"

Then the crowd of protestors broke into a chant, "Stop changing names! Stop changing names!"

The angry man interviewed, started another chant, "Fake Tears Chuck! Fake Tears Chuck!" All in the crowd joined with him on that chant.

"Oh brother!" said Karl, realizing the crazy had just taken over the sidewalk outside the White House fence.

As Sanders and Trump watched this interview and the chants began, the President turned to his press secretary and said, "You know they're right. They're dead right! I should have never changed the name. Why did you make me change it?"

Sanders feeling the accusatory tone pointed in her direction, quickly responded, "I was against the name change from the beginning if you recall, Mr. President."

"I don't," he said, pointing at her. "This was your fault. Yours alone."

"Sir you know I would always take responsibility for any mistakes I made, but if you recall it was Steve Bannon who suggested the change to 'Cryin' Chuck.' Remember, he said, two-word phrases are better than three."

"I don't recall that, but okay, it's Bannon's fault," Trump said, nodding his head. "So, we are putting the blame on Sloppy Steve. Is that right?"

"Squarely," said Sanders. "He's no longer here. He knows you're already angry with him for talking to that Fake News author Michael Wolff, so no question it was his fault and I think we should state that publicly, so everyone knows you didn't make the error."

"Nor did you?" asked Trump.

"There you go," smiled Sanders.

"I'm going out there, Sarah," said Trump. "Those are my people. I have to let them know that I support their protest and will set the record straight."

As six television news crews and several print and radio reporters weaved through the crowd of protestors, interviewing those who looked the craziest, one of the protestors yelled out, “There he is! President Trump!”

Despite their frustration over the President’s name change, the anger on the collective faces of the protestors quickly turned into wide bright smiles and cheers as they rushed toward the section of the fence where Trump and Sanders stood on the lawn, just a few feet from the fence with about a dozen Secret Service agents around them, weapons drawn. As Trump saw the tumultuous response from the crowd, he quickly flashed that all-too-familiar Trump smile and raised his arms straight out with two thumbs up.

“You’re the best!” he shouted to the crowd. “You’re my people, my supporters!”

The news crews tried to wedge their way through the tightly packed crowd, even knocking some people over, but had no success getting to the fence. Each of the network’s camera operators just held their twenty-thousand-dollar cameras as high as possible to get a shot of this incredible moment. The President of the United States walked right up to the fence to speak directly with a massive crowd of regular Americans, his loyalists, showing no fear at all, while each of the Secret Service agents surrounding him were pointing their pistols toward the crowd, looking for anyone who might look like a threat.

“Look, I just want you all to know that you are right!” he shouted, and the 5,000-plus protestors broke out into loud cheers.

“We are right! We are right!”

“Yes,” said Trump. “I should have never changed the name to Cryin’ Chuck.”

Another loud cheer erupted and voices yelling out, "Cryin' Chuck sucks! Cryin' Chuck sucks!"

"Yes, he does," the President continued. "As you know, I never admit to mistakes, but this is a very important issue, so I must admit to the mistake by Steve Bannon. It was all Sloppy Steve's fault!"

"Sloppy Steve sucks! Sloppy Steve sucks!" they chanted in unison.

"Yes, he does," agreed Trump. "So we are going back to the name I thought we should have kept, Fake Tears Chuck!"

"Fake Tears Chuck! Fake Tears Chuck!" was repeated for several minutes as T-shirts, caps and banners with 'Fake Tears Chuck' printed on them were held up high for all to see. The TV crews quickly recorded this mayhem but then turned back to Trump.

"We can't have a country where we call people hurtful names, and then for no reason, change those hurtful names. It will create confusion. After all, the new name may not be as hurtful, so there's that consideration. Given that, we can't allow some wealthy, loud-mouthed, egotistical idiot to decide that he wants to change the name in order to reduce it from three words to two. Am I right?"

A silence fell over the protestors who looked confused.

"I'm talking about Sloppy Steve!"

"Ohhhh!" and the cheers exploded louder than ever. "Sloppy Steve! Sloppy Steve! Sloppy Steve makes us heave!"

"Oh, I like that," said Trump. "Can I use it?"

"No!" yelled out Pateki holding up a T-shirt reading Sloppy Steve. "We've already got Sloppy Steve printed and warehoused."

"Got it," said The Donald. "So that concludes my impromptu meeting today with you, the people. My Trumpsters!"

Someone yelled out, “Mr. President, we love the names you call people!”

“Crooked Hillary! Crooked Hillary!” was voiced from one section, while “Rocket Man! Rocket Man!” was being chanted from another section and “Pocahontas! Pocahontas!” from the group closest to Trump.

“Thank you,” smiled Trump, giving two thumbs up again. “There are many important things that I have to take care of as President, but I view the name-calling and tweeting out angry comments as my priority. The people love it!”

The next day during Sanders's White House press briefing, the first question came from ABC White House correspondent Jonathan Karl. “Many of us covered the President speaking to the protestors outside of the White House fence yesterday. At what point does he realize that name calling is immature, hurtful, childish, and a bully tactic?”

Sanders opened the folded White House letterhead on the podium and said, “Well, the President in his infinite wisdom knew that would be the first question. And he also knew that I would call on you for the first question, so he crafted a very well-written Presidential response.”

Karl sat back down in his first-row seat, looking a bit nervous while CBS News's Major Garrett and FOX News's John Roberts, seated a few feet from him, turned toward him with a look that said, ‘You've just been set up.’ Karl felt like a reporter left on the tracks in front of a dark tunnel with the light from a train coming straight at him. He could feel the sweat pouring down his face as Sanders held up the paper to read it and said, “Here is the statement from the President regarding that question and I quote, “Bite me you bunch of losers! Especially you ABC and Jonathan Karl. Big bite! I have no respect for Fake News CNN, Fake News MSNBC,

Fake News CBS, NBC, ABC. Fake, faker, fakest. I watch them every day and don't recommend anyone watch them and their Fake News. I do however, highly recommend FOX News, especially *FOX and Friends* and Sean Hannity. Now those are real news reporters. But to this group, minus FOX, I would just like to repeat, bite me you bunch of losers!"

Sanders placed the paper back down on the podium as reporters' hands shot up, hoping to be called on to ask their question about this statement. Karl was more than a bit embarrassed and angry, having been singled out. He stood to ask a question, "Do you consider that a respectful response to the media? When has a President ever conducted himself this way?"

Sanders looked at Karl, flashed a smirk that dismissed his questions, then said, "That's all the time I have for questions today. Thank you."

And out the door the White House Press Secretary walked as Karl and several other reporters yelled out questions. From the doorway where Sanders had just exited, Trump's familiar voice was heard shouting out, "You bunch of losers! Bite me! You're all Fake News! Media Morons!"

CHAPTER 8

CHUCKY TODD AND THE SUNDAY MORNING TALKING HEADS

It was a typical Sunday morning during the first month of the new year and the talking heads on three of the four network morning shows were riled up over the news about President Donald Trump's attempt to have Special Counsel Robert Mueller fired the previous summer. According to reports, the White House Counsel Don McGahn threatened to resign if the President fired Mueller. Reportedly, at that point, Trump changed his mind and let it go.

Viewers across the country—liberals, independents, and conservatives—tuned in that Sunday to see the fireworks that would take place, as they knew the talking heads would be diving into this very controversial news; raising to the surface all of the most sensational items. The television remote control clickers would be working overtime as the over-fifty-crowd, the main audience for these four network shows, would be clicking up a storm, jumping back and forth between networks to make sure they didn't miss any of the juicy details. Those who were a little more technologically advanced, and actually knew how to record those shows, didn't have to sit there clicking like mad, knowing they could watch all three programs at their convenience. But in many homes across the country, old men wearing their pajamas or old favorite jeans which their wives had tried to throw out several times, were sitting in their favorite recliners, holding their clickers in one hand while sipping a mug full of coffee with the other.

Ah this was the life! For many men, watching controversial news, sipping coffee, and screaming at the television was better than watching the Super Bowl and drinking beer. For many wives, this became earplug Sunday; although some wives enjoyed sitting with their spouses and ranting right along with them at those liberal talking heads and double-talk politicians.

One of those elderly viewers, dressed in his satin blue jammies with cowboy images across the top, never missed a Sunday morning show. His thick locks of hair were neatly combed, as always, and his cozy, blue-felt slippers gave him the appearance of a well-dressed and well-groomed senior citizen. The smell of fresh ground coffee filled the living room where he sat in his favorite, ultra-comfortable brown leather recliner, complete with vibrating massage controls. He was already upset by the interview taking place on NBC's *Meet the Press* where Chuck Todd was interviewing former CIA Director, Robert Gates.

"You worked with Bob Mueller when he was head of the FBI," began Todd, who rose through the ranks of NBC News to host one of the most prominent shows. "What do you make of the President's attack on him? Do you have confidence in Bob Mueller? And if he were fired, how would you react?"

The old man in the recliner yelled at one of the four flat screen televisions on the wall in front of him, "You're an idiot Chuck Todd! An idiot! There was no attack on Mueller."

Gates answered the question saying, "I think Bob Mueller is a man of extraordinary character."

"Really?" said the old man, twitching his right slipper, irritated by the remarks.

"I can't think of anybody who would do a more honest and standup job conducting an investigation," continued Gates.

"I can think of a few," said the old man, who was suddenly interrupted by his young beautiful wife, dressed in pink-satin jammies with butterflies across the top and matching pink slippers.

"Donald, would you please stop yelling at the television," said Melania Trump, holding a cup of green tea. "They can't hear you."

The President looked at his wife, who sat in her brown leather recliner next to him.

"Well, they may not be able to hear me now, but they'll hear me later, plus I've got some tweets to send out here. And believe me, they'll hear those."

"Who are you yelling at?" asked Melania, sipping her tea.

"Chuck Todd, he's a moron," said the seventy-one-year-old Commander-in-Chief. "If someone threw a piece of cheese into the corner, I swear he'd scurry off to eat it between his two little paws. Rat-faced looking nerd! Oh, I've got a good name for him, Chucky Cheese."

Gates continued, "People are assuming he's going to come to one conclusion."

"I sure do," said the President. "No Russian collusion! None! Nada!"

"But people need to be prepared that a guy like Bob Mueller may come to a different conclusion that will elate some people and anger other people," said Gates. "I have total confidence in him."

"Well I don't," said Trump. "And if McGahn hadn't gotten in my way, Mueller would have been long gone. History baby! Do you hear me Chucky Cheese?"

Melania now listening to the interview turned to her husband and asked, "Donald, would you have fired him last summer?"

"In a New York minute baby!" said Trump, who began expertly typing a tweet with his index finger, to let the nation know his most current thoughts.

Chuck Todd is trying to create Fake News! I would have never fired Robert Mueller! And there was no Russian collusion. AND DAN SCAVINO DIDN'T WRITE THIS. I DID. DJT

The Tweeter-in-Chief hit send and, within seconds, Trump had thousands of likes, retweets, and replies, but mostly negative, as Trump twitter stalkers anxiously await his tweets to quickly respond and gain a top spot of recognition. His Twitter feed is the most followed and active account in the world, challenged only by Pope Francis, who has a slightly different message and doesn't receive hundreds and thousands of negative responses moments after he sends out a tweet.

Trump set down his new iPhone and picked up his gold-plated remote control to turn down Todd's interview and turn up ABC where Martha Radatz was filling in for George Stephanopoulos. She was interviewing South Carolina

Senator Lindsey Graham, who enjoyed a roller coaster ride of a relationship with the President.

"You said last Fall that any effort to go after Robert Mueller could be the beginning of the end for the Trump Presidency," began Radatz, a highly-respected veteran reporter at ABC News. "In light of the reporting that President Trump ordered the firing of Robert Mueller last June, backing down only when the White House Counsel threatened to resign, do you still believe what you said?"

With a very serious look on his face, the senator from South Carolina very directly stated, "Oh yeah, if he fired Mueller without cause, yes. Mueller's doing a good job. I have confidence in him to get to the bottom of all things Russia."

"I did not say I was going to fire Mueller," Trump yelled at the TV.

"But I thought you said you would fire him Donald," asked a puzzled Melania.

"Well yes, I'll tell you that classified top secret information. You're my wife," said Trump. "But not to them. It's classified. I would have fired him, pink-slipped him, hit the road Jack'd him. But that damn McGahn! Maybe I should have let him walk."

Graham continued, "And Don McGahn, if the story is true in *The New York Times*, then he did the right thing."

"Wrong!" barked Trump.

"And the good news is the President listened," said Senator Graham.

"I always listen. I'm a good listener, the best. Right Melania?"

"What?"

Graham continued, "I don't know if the story is true or not, but Mueller should look at it. I have complete confidence in Mr. Mueller."

"I don't!" yelped the President, with his wife looking on at this bipolar display of pure craziness.

Radatz continued with her line of questions, "So Senator Graham, do you believe the stories about McGahn and about President Trump?"

"I don't know," said Graham. "I believe it's something Mueller should look at. I'm not going to say it's Fake News and move on."

"I'm going to say it's Fake News and move on!" said Trump, who turned down the sound on Radatz and up on CBS TV's *Face the Nation*, while he began a new tweet.

Maratha Radatz, you're asking Lindsey Graham if he believes the New York Times story. Well here it is right from the top. No, it's not true. It's Fake News! I was never going to fire Robert Mueller. So there. End of story. And by the way, no Russian collusion. None!

Melania Trump couldn't stay silent and interjected, "Donald, why don't you just admit that you had thought about firing Robert Mueller but realized it was a mistake when Don McGahn made it clear to you and then decided not to fire him."

The President smirked at his wife, who was trying to help. "Melania, you've known me for a long time now. You know I never make mistakes. And when I do make mistakes, I never admit to them. And I most certainly never apologize for them. Why? Because the greatest cowboy to ever ride in the saddle, John Wayne, said in the movie, *She Wore a Yellow Ribbon*, and I quote, 'Never apologize, it's a sign of weakness.'"

"But you were going to fire Mueller," she said.

"Yes."

"But you are telling the world that you were not going to fire him."

"Right again."

"Well, aren't you lying to the world?" asked the very confused First Lady.

"I'm not lying," insisted her husband. "I don't lie. I am not a liar. I'm just positioning the information differently so everyone can understand it. You have to realize Melania, I'm a genius. I'm, like, a really smart guy, really smart. Not everyone can comprehend what I say."

"I don't understand what you say most of the time," said the immigrant from Slovenia, who earned great success as a fashion model and moved to New York, where she met real estate bigshot Donald Trump at a party at the Kit Kat Club in 1998.

"Because you're not a genius like me," said the always-humble Trumpster, looking at the screen showing *Face the Nation*. "But you're beautiful and I have big hands, so it's all good."

The President's eyes grew wide and his blood pressure shot sky high as he realized what he was looking at on the screen with the CBS show.

"Wait that's Nancy Cordes!" exclaimed The Donald. "She must be filling in for that John 'Dickhead' Dickerson? What the hell! Who picked her? Don't like her. She's a real Hillary cheerleader. Hates me. Loves the Clintons. I think she slept with Bill Clinton."

"What? You do?" Melania asked.

"No, but I think I should start that rumor on Twitter to get back at her for all the negative reporting she's done on me," snarled a revenge-filled Trump.

"That's a bad idea, Donald!" warned Melania. "She'll sue you."

"Okay, you're right. I won't."

Then Trump started typing with is index finger, but paused and deleted the tweet.

"Good call, Melania. That one might have gotten me into hot water."

Cordes was interviewing the White House Director of Legislative Affairs and Assistant to the President, Marc Short, about the same subject and asked, "Why did the President want to fire Special Counsel Mueller and why did he decide not to?"

"Well, Nancy, the President never intimated to me a desire to fire Mueller," explained Short.

"See, Short knows," Trump said proudly. "I never intimated to him. I don't even know what intimated means, but whatever it is, I didn't do it."

Short continued, "I think there's been a lot of sensational reporting on that. Let's keep in mind that the report dates to a June conversation. We are now in January. Mueller is still Special Counsel. Don McGahn is still running the White House Special Counsel's office. Millions of taxpayer dollars have been wasted on an investigation that so far has shown no collusion with the Russians."

"Well the investigation's not over," said Cordes.

"Well, of course not because it's continuing to drag on at great expense, yet no evidence of Russian collusion," said Short.

Trump stood up from his recliner and began clapping. "Yeah, yeah Marc Short! Now that's a great American. Maybe I should fire Mueller and make Marc Short the Special Counsel. He gets it. Gets it clearly. No Russian collusion!"

Short continued, "So, the reality is Mueller is still the Special Counsel, McGahn is still head of White House Counsel's office, and the President's never intimated to me a desire to fire Robert Mueller."

Trump walked over to his wife and gave her a high five. "How about that, Melania. Marc Short just hit it out of the park with that interview. Cleared it all up. That Cordes is a piece of work. I really need to tweet about her affair with Bill Clinton."

"But she didn't have one."

"I know. I know. The truth. It's always getting in my way."

Trump sat back in his ultra-comfortable recliner and turned his attention back to his Sunday morning news shows. His wife stood and said, "Donald, I have a speech to write for my address to a women's group tomorrow."

"Oh, that's good," said the President. "Do you know what you're going to write?"

"Not yet," said Melania. "I'm having my assistant pull some of Michelle Obama's speeches for inspiration."

"Oh, that's a good idea. You know there's a copy machine just down the hall."

"Yes, I know. Now I have to get to work. Writing is hard work."

"Copying too!" he added.

"Yes, it is," said Melania exiting out of the room, leaving her husband to watch Howard Kurtz on FOX News.

"Love this guy Kurtz. Tells it like it is. Exposes all the hypocrisy of the Fake News! Maybe I should make him Special Counsel."

CHAPTER 9

THE DAY MELANIA WARNED AMERICA

As the stock market hit record highs throughout 2017 and into the next year, the memory of what was taking place in America just ten years earlier seems somewhat of a distant memory for some. But for those who lived through it and survived it, *The Great Recession* was a time of great tragedy, when people were looking for answers. What would the future look like?

In one household in Bloomfield Hills, a very nice suburb of Detroit, a frustrated middle-aged businessman, Jim Sullivan, arrived at his home in the late afternoon of January 22, 2008, with the newspaper rolled up under his arm. The news that filled the pages of the *USA Today* on that cold, dark day couldn't have been worse. Unfortunately, it wasn't Fake News. Sullivan wondered if America would be able to rebound from all of the bad economic news that had so badly impacted the country only three months earlier.

Unemployment was high and growing. People were losing their homes to foreclosures at alarming rates. Divorces were up. A new war broke out between Israel and Hamas terrorists in the Gaza strip. The violence in the Afghanistan war was escalating. The American deficit was now in the trillions of dollars. A German billionaire threw himself in front of a train after his business empire ran into serious financial trouble.

All the while, the media kept everyone up to the minute on the fall of the world financial market and the great capitalistic society called America, which just led to more fear, doom, and gloom. But, as depressed as Jim felt, he knew one thing for certain. He would never consider ending the pain quickly like the man in Germany. He would get through it somehow.

When he walked through the door of his four-bedroom home, he was depressed and wondering how he would find a job to support his family of four. As he stood in the doorway, with his white dress shirt-tail hanging over his blue Men's Warehouse dress slacks, he admired his perfectly clean home with the smell of freshly baked cinnamon bread in the air. It was a wonderful home, a refuge from everything the world could throw at him.

His wife of twenty-seven years, Sally, a short, attractive, middle-aged mother of two children, was the perfect housewife, bringing warmth to the home that seemed only possible in fairytales. She was seated in her high-backed, red cloth armchair with a smile that lit her beautiful, olive-skinned, effervescent face as she watched a show on television. Jim set his black business case down, took off his smudged black wing-tips and walked over to see what was causing such delight. Surely she couldn't be watching the news.

From the kitchen, he could hear a familiar voice. It was Oprah Winfrey, the most popular and successful daytime talk show host in the history of television.

"Hello honey, I'm home," he greeted his wife, grimacing up the best smile he could muster under the circumstances.

"Quiet!" she said, holding up her right hand to hold back any further interruption.

"What?" asked Jim, not quite sure what was so important that his wife couldn't greet him.

"Don't you see," she said looking very upset. "Don't you see, Oprah can't get the weight off! It's horrible! I feel so bad for her. Her weight was down and now it's up again. Do you understand me?"

Jim looked a bit stunned at this revelation wondering why this was so important.

And there was Oprah, "I can't sleep!" said the megastar, who ten years later would consider running for President of the United States. "I lay there watching the clock. When you see me get heavy, it's not because I'm eating out of hunger. It's because my life is out of balance.

"I have a thyroid problem! Bob Greene said to me, you look like you have low-grade depression."

Bob Greene, an expert nutritionist whom Oprah made famous, had become very good friends with the superstar and on this day was seated next to her to give his account. "I looked at her eyes and she wasn't there," he said.

Jim stood there perplexed by the importance of this, when his wife turned to him and asked, "Did you hear that honey? She wasn't there. He looked into her eyes and couldn't find her."

"Yes, that's horrible," Jim said wondering how she could take this so seriously.

Green continued, "Oprah, I noticed that your movements were slower. There was something going on. You were not really there."

Oprah nodded in agreement and said, "I wasn't really there, was I, Bob? No, knew I needed help, needed something. My drug of choice was food. It used to be potato chips, but now it's organic multi-grain blue chips."

Sally was fascinated, "Hear that honey? Blue chips. Oprah loves the blue chips."

"I heard," responded Jim as Oprah continued her personal revelation.

"It all started when I stopped taking time for myself," she said. "I get unbalanced. Food is much more attractive to me at that time."

Jim just looked at his wife in amazement as she remarked, "Did you hear that? She wasn't taking time for herself. I don't take time for myself either."

"Yeah, you're just like Oprah," he said somewhat sarcastically, although Sally was too wrapped up in the program to pick up on it.

"I think I get unbalanced too," said Sally.

"I know you get unbalanced too," he said. "I also get unbalanced. What's for dinner?"

Her hand rose up to block the verbal intrusion. There was no time to consider anything except what was happening on the Sony Trinitron in the living room.

The camera moved in on Oprah, who had a look of new determination on her face. "This year, I'm going to have more joy, more balance in my life!"

"More joy, more balance. Hear that Jim?" said Sally while not taking her eyes off the set, her husband not wishing to comment for fear of starting an argument.

"I'm very hopeful," said Oprah. "We have to appreciate our life. Love ourselves."

"Jim, I need more balance. All I do is cook and clean and take care of the kids. I never take time for myself."

"You're right honey," agreed her loving husband. "When's dinner?"

Oprah continued, "My goal isn't to be thin, but to be the weight my body can hold. You have to plan your meals or you end up with blue chips."

"I'm not bringing blue chips in this house Jim," said Sally. "Do you hear me? Not going to do it!"

Jim looked puzzled, "Have we ever had blue chips here?"

"No, but I'm not going to start. Blue chips brought down Oprah. They're not going to get me. No sir."

"That's great! No blue chips," he said. "Take a stand. Beautiful!"

Jim looked at the newspaper he was holding in his right hand with the story of the billionaire who jumped in front of the train because he was so distraught over losing his fortune. Another story had a chart showing the downward direction of the economy with quotes from Wall Street experts saying they had never seen anything like this in America. Jim looked up at his wife enjoying the talk show, oblivious to the plight and pain of the world outside, completely focused on the pain her beloved Oprah was suffering. Jim couldn't take it any longer.

"Sally, I know how much you love Oprah, but can you try to gain some perspective here?" he began, knowing he was going down a tricky path, but with the first words out of his mouth, there was no turning back. "Oprah is a millionaire! She has people to cook for her. She has trainers to guide her in workouts to keep her fit and healthy. She will never have to worry about where her next dime is coming from, or her next meal for that matter. She's fine!"

Sally's face grew stern and her bottom lip began to quiver a bit. "How dare you, Jim! Oprah's in pain! She gaining weight and can't sleep. Her life is out of balance!"

Jim held up *USA Today*, "Did you see the front page of the paper today? A billionaire lost his empire and threw himself in front of a train. People are losing all of their money in the stock market, money they were counting on. And they're killing themselves over it. Killing themselves! Do you hear me?"

Sally's face dropped as she realized her husband's point. "I am very sorry to hear that, Jim. I know it's bad out there. Half our neighborhood is out of work and it seems a *For Sale* sign is popping up on another lawn nearly every day. I know it's bad. But that doesn't mean I shouldn't care about Oprah and her problems. Jim, she's out of balance for God's sake!"

The room grew quiet as the show came back from a commercial break. Jim sat in his recliner next to Sally and continued reading his *USA Today*. When Oprah returned, she was dressed in a sharp-looking grey dress from Gucci. She turned to her audience and said, "My next guest may be unfamiliar to some of you, but she is woman who came over from Europe and has built quite a successful life, someone you should know. Please welcome, Melania Trump."

The audience applauded as the camera panned across the ladies in their seats looking at a stunningly beautiful Melania Trump, a former fashion model dressed in a beautiful, bright red, mid-length dress by Dolce & Gabbana. She nodded her head to the audience in appreciation for their warm reception, then sat on the comfortable beige couch next to Oprah.

"Melania, you are obviously a very beautiful woman, married to real estate mogul Donald Trump," began Oprah, speaking about the man who had floated the idea of running for President. "Your husband, who is a good friend of mine, has done very well with his television show, *The Apprentice*."

"Yes, he has," agreed Mrs. Trump.

"But even with all of his success in real estate and on television, he continues to tell America that he may run for President of the United States," continued Oprah. "Now, I know the man and he wouldn't be able to put up with politicians, politics, and all of the crazy things that Presidents have to deal with on a daily basis."

"He would want to fire everyone," laughed Melania, lifting her right hand over her mouth to hide the hilarity she felt about the thought of her husband becoming President. "He loves firing people. Loves it!"

"Yes, I think we can agree that he is a man who wants things done his way every time," said Oprah.

"Every time," said Melania.

"Could you imagine if he actually became President?" Oprah chuckled at the ludicrous thought. "He would have the entire country up in arms. First of all, I don't know what party he would run under, but whichever one it was, I can promise you that the senators and representatives of that party wouldn't like it."

"No, no, they would not," said Melania. "He would tell them all what to do, and if they didn't listen to him, he would start bullying them and calling them names."

"He would?" asked Oprah, not familiar with that side of The Donald. "Donald can be a bully? And uses name-calling?"

"Oh yes," said Melania. "He loves bullying, pushing people around, attacking them by calling them names."

"Oh my!" said Oprah, quite surprised by this revelation. "I never knew. Does he not see how childish and immature that is, not to mention the bullying?"

"No, he just likes to get his way and will do whatever it takes—bully, lie, connive," laughed Melania.

"Oh my goodness. Well, how do you put up with that type of behavior, Melania?" Oprah asked.

"Oh, well that's easy," said Melania, whose maiden-name is Knauss and married one of New York's most famous celebrities in 2005. "When I married him, he insisted on a prenuptial agreement, but I insisted on a few things in that prenup that will make me a very wealthy woman, once I say *adios* to the lunatic. I believe in this country they would say that I've hit the jackpot or won the lottery, right?"

"Right, easy street to be sure," said Oprah. "But Melania, no offense, but when most people hear that your husband might run for President, they think it's a joke. They say, and these are not my words, that he is a clown, someone who is starving for attention."

"I believe that is a pretty good assessment," said Melania, not taking into consideration how this interview would hurt her husband if he actually did run. "He spends a good two hours a day in front of the mirror, not only to try and comb that disaster on top of his head, but just because he can't get enough of himself. He loves himself."

"Do you love him?" asked Oprah.

Melania bent over laughing, then looked at Oprah and said, "Did you hear the part about the prenup and becoming a wealthy woman?"

"Well Melania, I have to tell you what a lot of people in America have said about you, and again not my words, but they say that you are a gold-digger. They look at you and it's quite apparent that you are much younger than Donald, twenty-four years younger! You are beautiful and he is very wealthy."

The smile on Melania's face dropped and she said quite sternly to Oprah, "I am not a gold-digger. I have never used a shovel in my life. When I moved to New York, my goal was to become one of the most famous fashion models in the world."

"To perhaps be cast in movies or television shows?" Oprah asked.

"No, to get some ego-driven millionaire, who doesn't have the intelligence of a third grader, to propose to me, so I could cash in on his stupidity," she said.

"But that is a gold-digger," said Oprah.

"Well, I consider it a gold-collector, no digging involved."

Jim and Sally, sat in their respective chairs, watching this display of craziness. Jim turned to his wife and said, "Well, I have to say Sally, I think you're right about Oprah. I promise you that I would have never learned anything like this by reading *The New York Times* or *USA Today*. This is unbelievable!"

Sally stood and walked over to her husband, sitting on his lap and hugging him as he shifted the recliner back.

"The good news is," continued Jim, holding his loving wife in his arms. "We'll never have to worry about her Bozo husband becoming President of the United States."

"Could you imagine Donald Trump as President of the United States?" asked Sally, laughing.

"Not in a million years!" exclaimed Jim. "The day Donald Trump is President of the United States is the day I look out the window and see a blue moon."

"Well, I hope that day never comes," said Sally.

"The only way a guy like Trump could ever win the Presidency is if someone who the majority of Americans absolutely hated, absolutely deplored, ran against him; someone so corrupt and dishonest..."

"Like Hillary Clinton?" asked Sally.

"Oh, she would never do that again," said Jim. "She just lost to a man who became the first black President, something all the experts said could never happen this soon. Not even Hillary, with her ego and ambition, would attempt to go through that again."

"Could you imagine, Trump versus Clinton for President in 2016?" laughed Sally with her husband clapping in delight at such a crazy notion.

"Not even Hollywood could dream up that nightmare scenario," said Jim. "Plus, they would both be in their seventies. The only thing crazier than that would be if that independent Senator from Vermont, Bernie Sanders, were to run. He keeps talking about it, but he would be seventy-four."

"That's hilarious," said Sally. "How would an old man like that ever expect to get the young voters behind him?"

"Never happen," said Jim, looking back at the television where Oprah had a very concerned look on her face.

"So, Melania, tell us, if your husband became President of the United States someday, how would he conduct himself?" asked Oprah.

Melania's eyebrows raised at the proposed thought, but seemed to know the answer saying, "Well, he has actually talked about this quite a bit at our home. Not to me of course, but to some of his business associates. He has said that he would get rid of all the regulations that are holding companies back and allow business people to do whatever they pleased to make money."

"Doesn't that open the door wide for corruption?" asked Winfrey.

"You would assume," answered the always polite Melania. "He said he would get rid of all of the environmental protections too. And he said he would build up the military, like no-one has ever seen before, and go after some of those countries that have been taking advantage of America."

A very serious look crossed Winfrey's face as she turned to the camera and said, "Well we can all be thankful that Melania's husband is doing so well in real estate and with *The Apprentice* that he would never have the time to run for President."

Melania just smiled and Oprah went to a commercial break as Jim turned off the television. "Can you believe that, Sally?" laughed Jim at the absurd idea of Donald Trump someday becoming President. "It would be a pretty scary world if Donald Trump ever became President."

Sally was busy reading something on her iPhone.

"Jim, I just googled blue moon," Sally said, pointing her index finger toward some information on the phone. "And according to this, there is actually supposed to be a blue moon on January 31, 2018."

The couple just looked at each other for a moment, then busted out laughing.

"No way, no way!" chortled Jim. "Hey, check to see if Hell is supposed to freeze over that day as well. Then we'll know we're in trouble."

CHAPTER 10

DAZZLING FOX NEWS BEAUTY DECKS MSNBC RIVAL

Bill O'Reilly is a longtime media professional, who President Donald Trump does not consider Fake News, but a reliable resource for his insight and strategic recommendations regarding his dealings with the mainstream news media—those whom Trump does consider Fake News. O'Reilly would have been enjoying that recognition among conservatives and independents, if he had not crossed the sexual harassment line over and over again, thinking he could pay his way out of potential lawsuits each time.

Before O'Reilly became famous for his inappropriate conduct at FOX News, he was America's most successful prime time news commentator. His weekday news program, *The O'Reilly Factor*, had 3.5 million viewers each evening and he maintained his position as the *King of News Talk* for more than fifteen years on FOX News. He came off as a tough guy on the set, and we learned from legitimate news reports that he was quite a bully off the set as well. He manipulated women he was attracted to, using his power to book them on his television show or claim he could get them hired at FOX, as his bargaining chips.

During O'Reilly's rise to fame, around the time when Barack Obama became President of the United States, one of his biggest detractors was MSNBC's prime time ultra-liberal commentator, Keith Olbermann. The tall, out-of-shape, left-wing news star was best known as a sports anchor on ESPN who was hired by MSNBC to spout off his very liberal and very critical opinions about anything conservative. Sports fans knew Olbermann for his witty and tough commentary which drew him a fan base that he somehow parlayed into the news/talk gig. The transition took him into a more respected realm of American society—serious television news commentary. But his opinions off the set with MSNBC staffers and executives got him into trouble and he was shown the door.

Since his departure from the cable news network, he bounced around from network to network, finally landing on a web-based show for *GQ* where he read the April 19, 2017, *New York Times* story about O'Reilly being fired for his bullying and sexual harassment controversy. This may have been Olbermann's happiest day, as he picked up the phone and called his arch-nemesis. To the ultra-liberal know-it-all's surprise, O'Reilly took his call, while he was packing up his desk. The former *King of News Talk* was not in a very good mood as he lit into the grinning liberal with no holds barred on his language or the volume-level of his voice.

Olbermann, who could never be accused of being anything resembling a tough guy, given his lack of coordination and athletic ability, felt his grin harden to clenched teeth, becoming so angry on the phone that he challenged O'Reilly to a fight.

O'Reilly didn't have to be asked twice and was looking forward to tattooing Olbermann with every ounce of hate he was feeling for those whom he felt had unfairly brought him down. Over the next few weeks, their agents worked with Sylvester Stallone to plan a three-round boxing match to take place in Yankee Stadium. Here is the untold story of what took place on July 15, 2017.

❧

It was a hot Saturday in Yankee Stadium, where a boxing ring was set up on the outfield grass just behind second base, so everyone in the sold-out, 54,000-seat stadium had a good view. Unlike the previous boxing matches held in the original Yankee Stadium, the air is not filled with smoke, exuding from the thick cigars clenched between the teeth of men, wearing straw hats in June of 1938, hoping that Joe Louis would win for America and beat Germany's Max Schmeling in this rematch from 1936.

No, on this day the stands were filled with neatly dressed men in white-collared shirts, khaki pants, polished shoes, and neatly combed hair. That was the section rooting for "Battling Bill" O'Reilly, who was favored against his hated opponent, Keith "The Big Oaf" Olbermann, in a three-round bout to determine who was the real news talk champion.

ESPN, *The Big Oaf's* former employer, was broadcasting the event live. Chris "Back, Back, Back" Berman was doing the play-by-play, with former middleweight champion Sugar Ray Leonard providing the color commentary.

The two preliminary bouts featured right-wing commentator Ann Coulter against morning talk show host Joy Behar, which went the full three rounds in a bloody and ferocious battle that was scored a draw.

The next match pitted conservative FOX News and national radio talk show host Sean Hannity against CNN cable television news host Anderson Cooper, who surprisingly won the first two rounds easily, but was knocked out with just thirty seconds left in the final round, when Hannity threw a hard right hook to Cooper's soft left cheek.

As with all major fights, a buzz filled the air, the crowd excited to see these two talk show giants throw real jabs and punches instead of the barbs they had traded over the air. Minnesota Senator Al Franken, who would resign from Congress five months later after a host of embarrassing sexual harassment allegations were revealed about him, was introduced to the crowd and jumped up into the ring waving to all. If O'Reilly were to win, Franken promised to be his next opponent. O'Reilly really wanted a crack at Franken, who looked like the kind of guy *The Big Oaf* would have hung around with in college. This was the classic battle of the jocks versus the dweebs, but the dweebs had a forum to display their quick wit and intelligence, which is really all that matters on the tube.

"I'm a Senator!" yelled Franken at O'Reilly's fans seated around the ring, as security guards asked him to step down and sit down. "I'm calling the shots, not you! Because I'm Al Franken!"

Bill O's fans stood and booed the munchkin-looking politician, throwing wadded-up paper and smashed paper cups, anything they could find to hurl at him as he was led out of the ring.

At that moment, Keith Olbermann came out of the third base dugout onto the field of the most famous Major League team in the world. For a vociferous fan like Olbermann, that was an incomparable thrill, a moment he would always remember. As his handlers led him up the steps, thunderous applause was heard from the left-field stands, where some of his fans held their beer in one hand while trying to clap for their hero.

The Big Oaf fan section resembled a scene at a Pink Floyd concert, with funny little cigarettes being passed around from one long-haired, skinny, dirty-looking freak to the next liberal mumbling the words, "Good stuff man!" Mixed in throughout the crowd were two familiar faces—Sean Penn and Tim Robbins. They were easy to identify in this section of left-field liberals, because they were seated together with a red velvet rope surrounding them and two large, muscular security guards standing on each side of the improvised VIP section.

"I love you, Sean," yelled one adoring admirer, a thin well-dressed man who tried to reach past the security guard to touch pop singing star Madonna's ex-husband. "I'm a commie and your biggest fan!"

"I love you too," snarled Penn with great affection, then whispered to the guard, "If he comes over the rope, let him have it." Penn smiled widely at his fan and waved. "I'm one of you; one of the people."

The police purposely divided the crowd according to whom they were rooting for in this fight. They expected more and better fights in the stands than would take place in the ring this evening, but they worked to keep the two sides apart. The cops had O'Reilly winning by ten to one odds.

Back on the field, the *Countdown Assassin*, the nickname Olbermann created for himself, stood in front of the third base dugout, looking up at his adoring fans and raising his left fist high to signal that he was ready to take on his foe. A louder applause filled the stadium and several beers fell over the wall onto the field, one splashed onto the head of a fifty-nine-year-old security guard named Al Smith.

The *Countdown Assassin* was evident on the back of Olbermann's royal-blue robe with white and red trim, as he walked toward the ring. No matter what nickname he tried to promote, his fans knew him best as *The Big Oaf.* He was accompanied by his former associates at MSNBC, Chris Matthews and Rachel Maddow, who agreed to work his corner. Why they agreed to help Olbermann was a mystery, as he had a history of being rude and obnoxious to his co-workers at the network and everywhere else he worked. Whispers of speculation filled the left-field stands, but most centered on the cable network's need for publicity and they saw this as an opportunity.

The *Countdown Assassin* walked directly up the three stairs to the ring, squeezed between the ropes, and stepped onto the white canvas where his bow-legged gait was quickly recognized, identifying him as a real geek. A hush crossed the left-field bleachers as, for the first time, his fans realized that their hero may not be able to physically backup the shots he has taken at O'Reilly through the many years.

Just then, O'Reilly was seen emerging from the first base dugout, the home team's dugout, the Yankees' dugout. He was wearing a very bright red, white, and blue robe. The well-dressed contingent in the right-field stands boomed their approval, setting down their glasses of scotch, martinis, and fine white wine to cheer for exactly ten seconds, before sitting back down to finish their beverages of choice. "Bravo! Bravo, ol' sport!" was heard from the stands. Those are the "folks" whom O'Reilly always referenced on his show.

A serious and determined O'Reilly walked toward the ring and up the steps, confidently moving through the ropes and then around the ring with right hand upraised, as he glared at Olbermann, who displayed that all-too familiar smirk on his face, as if to say, "Give me a break!"

O'Reilly spotted Senator Al Franken in the crowd and walked to the ropes closest to him, leaned over, and yelled, "You're next, you Franken idiot! You're next!" Franken's face crinkled into a laughing smirk as he flipped off his detractor.

Unlike Olbermann, O'Reilly brought in a real boxing expert with highly respected trainer Joe Gallagher working his corner.

FOX newswoman Kimberly Guilfoyle, a beautiful conservative commentator, was scheduled to split the ring card duties with MSNBC's *Morning Joe* co-host, Mika Brzezinski, a very attractive newswoman who was probably in better shape than anyone in the stadium, due to her five-mile-a-day running routine. Given the many sexual harassment allegations and lawsuits against O'Reilly by several newswomen at FOX, no one could understand why Guilfoyle would agree to the ring card duties, but whispers of speculation filled the Yankee Stadium right-field stands.

THE FIGHT

A distinguished-looking man in a black tux and bow tie, full head of gray hair, and shined black shoes entered the ring, shook hands with the contenders, and reached up with his right hand to grab the microphone being lowered from the rafters. Famed ring announcer, Michael Buffer, spoke into the mic, "Good evening ladies and gentlemen and welcome to the main event. Tonight, we have with us two heavyweights of the news business, two dynamic personalities, two men who look just a tad out of shape in their boxing shorts. Yes, these two men have been at each other's throats over the airwaves for several years and tonight they have entered the ring to settle this dispute, like men, once and for all. And tonight, we will find out if either one of them can throw a punch as well as they throw a verbal jab.

"Now let me introduce them to you. In the left corner of the ring, standing six feet, three and one-half inches tall, weighing two hundred and twenty-five pounds, and wearing blue shorts with a red and white stripe down the side, long black socks, and retro Converse All-Star shoes, Keith 'Countdown Assassin' OLBERMANN!!!!!!"

The crowd in the left-field seats jumped to their feet and roared their approval with a loud ovation, chanting, "Big Oaf! Big Oaf! Big Oaf!" Olbermann looked over at them very disappointed that his preferred nickname didn't take hold with his fans.

"And in the right corner," continued Buffer. "Standing six feet, four inches tall, weighing in at two hundred and twenty pounds, and wearing white shorts with red and blue stripes, 'Battling Bill' O'Reilly!!!!!"

The men who filled the right- and center-field stands rose to their feet in a dignified manner, clapping and cheering, "Bill O! Bill O! Bill O!" O'Reilly looked up at his crowd disappointed they would support him with the term Olbermann used to mock him.

"The referee for tonight's contest is Sylvester Stallone."

The entire stadium began chanting, "Rocky! Rocky! Rocky!"

Buffer then sang out, "Now ladies and gentlemen, let's get ready to R-U-M-B-L-E!!!!!" The song *Whoomp There It Is* began blaring over the sound system with seemingly everyone in the stands dancing, clapping, and yelling.

In front of them, the two contenders stepped to the middle of the ring, where another stare down took place as the referee went over the rules.

"Okay, yo, look here, this will be a fair fight," said Stallone, who put the match together and elected to take on the referee duties as well, despite the objections of both contenders. "No grabbing and holding, no kicking, no hitting below the belt or behind the back. You know what I mean? Huh? You got it?"

The two men nodded as snarls crossed their respective faces.

"Yo, now as for trash talking, there will be no sexual innuendo, no remarks that could be deemed as sexual harassment. Do we understand each other Mr. O'Reilly?"

O'Reilly quickly responded, "Of course!"

Olbermann just laughed and Stallone rolled his eyes, "Right. And no gay jokes, no metaphorical references to your opponent's relationship with his mother, if you know what I mean."

Olbermann interrupted, "How about ugly jokes?"

"Absolutely! Good ugly jokes though," said Stallone. "I don't want to hear any of those, yo' mama's so ugly...you know what I mean?"

O'Reilly interrupted, "Fat jokes! What about fat jokes?"

"Definitely. And I got a couple good ones in case you run out. Now touch gloves, go to your corner, and come out fighting at the bell. That's when it rings, you know?"

O'Reilly held up his gloves and Olbermann smacked them down hard, sneering at the fallen cable news star, who was trying to resurrect his career via a podcast and website.

"Nice sneer," said Stallone. "I like that. You and him, start punching."

Just as O'Reilly turned and walked toward his corner to begin the bout, Olbermann waved for the microphone to be brought down. It was lowered before O'Reilly reached his corner. The crowd gasped wondering what was happening. The *Countdown Assassin* took the mic between his two boxing gloves and said:

"Hi this is Keith Olbermann from the highly-rated *GQ* webcast."

A huge laugh exploded from the right-field stands while Tim Robbins and Sean Penn covered their ears. "I am ready to kick Bill O's butt right here, right now!" yelled Olbermann. "Are you ready to see it?"

A burst of applause came from left field and was quickly followed by loud boos from the right- and center-field seats. O'Reilly turned to watch this egomaniacal display with a look of disgust across his face. He marched toward the center but was cut off by Stallone, who grabbed the microphone from Olbermann and said directly into it so all could hear, "Yo, one more rule. No trying to talk your way out of this fight, you know?"

Cheers came from the right-field stands as *The Big Oaf* frowned then shouted toward O'Reilly, "You are the worst person in the world today! No, the worst person of the year!"

From left field came applause; right field, boos.

The two news stars walked to their respective corners where their cornerman took their robes. O'Reilly made the sign of the cross just as the bell rang and went into a boxer's stance, with left glove forward and right glove close to his right cheek. Olbermann walked toward the middle of the ring with arms at his sides looking extremely bow-legged with each stride. A look of concern crossed Sean Penn's face as he looked over at Tim Robbins, whose eyes grew wide as he shrugged his shoulders indicating he didn't know that their left-wing news hero was such a dork.

As O'Reilly drew close, Olbermann put his two gloves up in front of him to block any punches coming toward his face. O'Reilly threw two quick jabs at *The Big Oaf*'s head which knocked him back a bit, then threw a hard right at his mid-section which landed in what looked like a sea of jelly as it absorbed the punch. The *Countdown Assassin*'s gloves came down and he looked like he was about to present his lunch to *Battling Bill.* But Bill O didn't have time for lunch, regurgitated or not. He threw a quick left jab at Olbermann's nose and hard right to his cheek. *The Big Oaf* staggered back as his mouthpiece flew up in the air and onto the canvas.

"Now why don't you show me how tough you are, you pansy!" snapped Bill O. "You can dish it out on the air but now you have to take it, you pinhead! Why don't you tell me I'm the worst person in the world again, huh?"

O'Reilly was riled up and quickly descended upon Olbermann, throwing a combination of hard punches, connecting to *The Big Oaf*'s face and mid-section several times. The final blow, a hard right to the mouth, sent the *Countdown Assassin* to the canvas for his real countdown.

O'Reilly strutted to the far corner with a satisfied smirk across his face knowing he had finally gotten the chance to do to his greatest news enemy what he had been dreaming about for years. Olbermann fan Tim Robbins, thinking his champ had been quickly slaughtered, shook hands with his pal Sean Penn and headed for the exit.

Stallone stood over the fallen newsman counting, "Okay yo, like one, two, three…" throwing his right hand toward him with index finger pointed with each count. O'Reilly used the moment to yell at Al Franken in the crowd. "Hope you're ready for some of this, Al Franken, you idiot!" The Minnesota senator again saluted him with his middle finger.

"There's a fine upstanding political leader," smacked O'Reilly, smirking at the man he really wanted to fight in the ring.

When Stallone reached six, Olbermann began to recover and managed to get up to his feet just before the count went to ten. With blood dripping from his nose, right eye swollen, and bottom lip cut, he didn't look beaten. No, he looked mad. From his corner Rachel Maddow yelled, "Get him, Keith. Get him for all of us who have been beaten up and picked on by bullies. Get him!"

With new determination, Olbermann walked toward O'Reilly, who looked shocked.

"You want some more?" snapped O'Reilly and quickly went back into his boxing stance. "Fine, you pinhead. I've got plenty more to give you." As Olbermann moved closer, he reached back with his right hand, like a baseball pitcher winding up to throw the hardest pitch he could muster at his news nemesis, who should have ducked, because the punch found its way over O'Reilly's boxing gloves and landed squarely on his nose, sending him flying backward, bouncing off the ropes and falling flat on his face, smashing against the canvas. Just as he hit the deck, the bell sounded ending the first round.

The senator from Minnesota stood up and yelled at O'Reilly, who could clearly see him under the ropes, "Yeah, I want some of that you buffoon. I want all of that Bill O!" A surprised Tim Robbins stopped at the exit ramp to see if his media buddy might actually win.

O'Reilly rose slowly to his feet muttering something about his wish to go to a commercial break. He walked rather unsteadily toward his corner, where his stunned-looking trainer placed his stool down, which the six-foot four-inch former King of News Talk plopped down upon, just as a metal bucket appeared in front of him.

O'Reilly glared across the ring. He didn't like being embarrassed in front of the entire nation watching the fight on ESPN as well as all of his peers and enemies sitting ringside. He thought he had an easy victory. But now he knew Olbermann was not going down without a fight. And a fight O'Reilly was going to give him. That bell may have ended the first round, but in O'Reilly's mind, it signaled the end of the fight for *The Big Oaf*, who he would not treat so nicely in the next round.

Just then, the ring-card girl entered through the ropes. It was the magnificent FOX News's host Kimberly Guilfoyle, dressed in a short, tight, lowcut royal blue dress with shimmering nylons over her long legs and sparkling blue high heels, the same type of attire she wore on FOX News's *The Five* each weeknight. She sauntered around the ring holding up the round card number '2'. O'Reilly just looked at her, wondering what she was doing there, well aware that FOX News was working to distance the network from him. He knew Stallone would have been the one to hire her.

"Wow! Would you look at that?" said Stallone to no one in particular as he watched the stunning beauty circle the ring. As she passed Olbermann, the dazzling ring lady paused right in front of him and her bright smile quickly turned to a wild-eyed look on her face, as she yelled, "You slimeball! You're going down. If he doesn't knock you out, I will. And believe me, I can!"

Stallone rolled his eyes and turned away saying, "Well, didn't see that coming. Must really hate that guy."

Olbermann looked up at the angry ring card lady, while Rachel Maddow wiped the blood from his nose and mouth. "Hey, any men left working at FOX or have they all been fired for sexual harassment?" Olbermann shouted toward the FOX brunette bombshell, who knew how sore that subject was for all those still employed at the number one rated cable network.

Guilfoyle became enraged, an angry snarl filling her once pretty face as she dropped the card and lunged toward Olbermann, who tried holding her back with both of his gloves outstretched. Maddow jumped between them, grabbed Guilfoyle and threw the angry conservative newswoman to the canvas, but she popped right back up and jumped into a boxer's stance, as did Maddow.

It was round one for the unscheduled bout. The two famous television news journalists threw lefts and rights as Stallone hurried to get between them, raising his arms, hoping to separate the two angry ladies. Before he could fully raise his arms however, he was hit with a left cross by Maddow and right hook by Guilfoyle. Sylvester Stallone went down like a ton of bricks. The two women moved around him and continued their fight.

"C'mon, you obnoxious, over-rated liberal. I'll kick your ass!" screamed Guilfoyle.

"Yeah, bring it, you attention-getting leg exhibitionist!" snapped Maddow.

"Yeah, why don't you tell me about Donald Trump's scandalous tax returns first," said Guilfoyle, really angering Maddow, resurrecting one of her most embarrassing reports.

Olbermann stood up, not knowing what to do, but saw a vendor near the ring. "Hey, can I get a beer here. This could be a great fight."

Just then, Guilfoyle threw a hard right which connected with Maddow's chin, sending her to the mat, lying right next to Stallone. The tall, older, bow-tied man working the bell began ringing it nonstop, as several boxing officials crawled through the ropes and grabbed the two women, taking them out of the ring as the shaken Stallone was helped to his feet.

MSNBC's *Morning Joe* co-host, Mika Brzezinski, was standing next to the now lone cornerman, Chris Matthews, watching all of this craziness. As the next ring-card girl, she too was looking quite spectacular, dressed in a very respectable red mid-length dress and matching red high heels, with her left hand on her hip, and right hand holding the 'Round 3' card. She turned to Matthews and asked with great concern, "I thought the ring girls just walked around the ring holding up the card. Do I have to fight someone from FOX?"

Matthews smiled and joked, "Yeah, Sean Hannity, and I'll bet you can take him too! Hah!"

Stallone, now bandaged up, stepped back to the middle of the ring, where he motioned for the two fighters to join him.

"Yo, look!" he said, quite angry. "The whole country may be watching this fight and we would like to conduct it in an organized fashion, you know? If any of your cornermen come out here and start fighting, I'll stop this bout and you can go outside the stadium to settle your differences. Understand?"

Olbermann and O'Reilly nodded.

"Now go to your corners and come out fighting at the bell. That's when it rings, you know?"

"We know!" said O'Reilly and Olbermann in unison to the beloved referee. Then O'Reilly, with a look of great anger across his face, snapped at Olbermann. "I'm not taking it easy on you anymore! Your next stop is Mount Sinai Hospital."

Olbermann was none too happy himself and fired back, "We'll see about that, asshole!"

The bell rang and the two fighters jumped out quickly to the middle of the ring. This time, *The Big Oaf* set up in a traditional boxer's stance, as did O'Reilly. Olbermann threw two left jabs, which O'Reilly easily batted aside with his left hand, then threw a hard right, which the *Oaf* ducked.

Tim Robbins came back to his seat from the exit ramp where he had been standing since the first round, thinking this would be a quick fight.

Olbermann, trying to imitate Muhammad Ali's athletically-beautiful style of boxing, danced quite awkwardly to his left, throwing left jabs at the head of O'Reilly, who held his ground, standing straight up, looking like Joe Louis. Olbermann looked so silly trying to box like Ali that O'Reilly's anger melted and he began to laugh. That was quickly erased as *The Big Oaf* connected with a left hand to the right cheek of Bill O, who retaliated by rushing at him like a bull, throwing him against the ropes in the corner and hitting him with a combination of lefts and rights, as Olbermann tried to cover up with his gloves to survive the onslaught.

"Forty seconds," yelled Gallagher, indicating to his fighter how much time was left in the round. Tim Robbins got up from his seat again and started up the steps. O'Reilly's flurry was hurting his opponent, but at the same time, he was tiring himself out. It wasn't quite the Rope-A-Dope, but it seemed to have the same result. A spent O'Reilly backed off, trying to catch his breath. Olbermann was hurt and not able to attack. The crowd yelled for the kill, but neither man could react. Twenty seconds on the clock.

Stallone stood to the side watching this pathetic sight, "Are you kidding me with this? Bring back the ladies. At least they can fight."

Mika Brzezinski heard him and thought he was serious. She stepped up next to the ropes, preparing to enter the ring as a few political leaders seated ringside began whistling at her to show their appreciation for her beauty. A middle-aged usher asked one of them, former President Bill Clinton, to stop the harassment, but allowed the politician seated next to him, Hillary, to continue with her wolf calls toward Mika.

It seemed O'Reilly and Olbermann were content to let the final twenty seconds tick off the clock when *The Big Oaf* decided to explode from his corner and threw the most awkward looking combination of punches at *Battling Bill*, who was able to get his hands up to protect his face until the bell rang.

Both men, looking very tired, returned slowly to their corners. Stallone could only watch in amazement, but smiled when he saw the new ring girl enter through the ropes, and once again said to no one in particular, "Yeah, that's what I'm talking about!"

The beautiful and fit Mika Brzezinski was helped through the ropes by none other than President Clinton who said, "Here you go Mika, just bend down and crawl through there."

The petite news lady tried to maintain her composure under such strange circumstances and bent over to crawl through the ropes, avoiding the former Commander in Chief's groping hands before he could assist her too much.

"Yeah baby! Yeah!" was heard coming loudly from the crowd behind them to which the ex-President turned and yelled, "Would you knock it off Hillary!"

Brzezinski walked around the ring holding her third round card high, showing off the very nice figure of this veteran news woman and mother of two. Her fiancé, Joe Scarborough, watched with pride from ringside seats. She passed Olbermann, who was panting heavily as he sat on the stool, now being attended by a professional boxing cornerman, who was appalled at the job the amateur, Matthews, had been doing. *The Big Oaf* sat there having water sponged onto his bleeding, sweating face and was actually starting to believe he could win the fight.

In the other corner, Gallagher worked furiously on O'Reilly, placing an oxygen mask over his face to help him recuperate. "Get ready Bill, they are about to ring the bell," said the longtime trainer, taking the oxygen mask and pulling the stool back between the ropes. "This is it. You must win this round. Go for the knockout."

Both O'Reilly and Olbermann looked determined as they glared across the ring at each other. "If I don't win this," said O'Reilly, "May I die right here in the ring."

Olbermann overheard him and said to his cornerman loudly enough for O'Reilly to hear, "If I don't win this, may O'Reilly die right here in the ring." Then *The Big Oaf* turned to his new cornerman and gave him a high five, "Pretty good huh! That's why I am so popular baby."

The bell rang and out sprang the two legendary newsmen ready to put their careers and lives on the line in this third and final round.

All of a sudden, they each seemed to find a new energy and determination, not to mention a set of boxing skills no one could have imagined each man possessed.

O'Reilly struck first with a combination of lefts and rights to the Olbermann's head and mid-section that sent the quipster back a bit, but he was unfazed. He came charging right back at O'Reilly, swinging wildly at him, and connected with a long right hand that looked like it came from the Bronx and landed in Queens—Queens being O'Reilly's left eye.

O'Reilly was hurt by the shot, but retaliated with another series of blows to Olbermann's head that brought the crowd to its feet watching to see if liberal America's champion would fall. Not a chance, he swung back hard with a left to hit O'Reilly in the mid-section, then followed with a right cross catching his nose and finished with a flurry of punches that O'Reilly was able to block. "Forty seconds," yelled Gallagher, letting conservative America's fallen news king know that he had better go for the knockout because he might be behind on points.

With every ounce of energy he could muster, the *Countdown Assassin* threw punch after punch trying to create a spin zone in O'Reilly's head, but the tall Irishman wasn't going to settle for a win on points. No, he wanted the knockout. As *The Big Oaf* threw another long right hand, *Battling Bill* hit him in the gut, hard, with a short quick left that caused Olbermann to lean forward, as he tried to protect himself. O'Reilly followed with a right upper cut to the *Oaf's* exposed chin that connected hard sending him backwards, falling, and landing on the canvas. Once again Stallone was over Olbermann counting, "Yo, like one, two, three...."

O'Reilly walked to the opposite corner ready to come out again in case his loud-mouthed liberal opponent survived his final countdown. But not this time as Stallone finished, "eight, nine, ten. You're out!"

O'Reilly raised his right glove in victory as the theme song from the movie *Rocky* was heard throughout the arena. The right- and center-field stands roared filling the stadium with a thunderous applause, as Al Franken quickly scampered toward the exit. Tim Robbins was already on his way to the airport.

Just then, the music was cut off and the vivacious Guilfoyle was seen at center ring holding a microphone and yelled out, "Get him girls!"

Before he knew what hit him, literally, Bill O'Reilly watched five of the FOX newswomen, whom he had harassed and paid off for their silence, stream into the boxing ring. Wearing boxing gloves and headgear, they were led by Andrea Mackris and Andrea Tantaros, running toward O'Reilly with a look of extreme anger and determination on their collective faces. Upon reaching the former *King of News Talk*, they began throwing punches at his head, stomach, and yes, especially O'Reilly's anchor desk, which caused a real spin zone in the Long Island Irishman's head. He fell backwards to the mat and was clearly out cold. The women stood over him, each placing their right pink Nike athletic shoe on his chest and raising their respective right arm in victory. A photo of that moment would be published on the cover of *TIME* Magazine.

"This is for all the women who have been bullied and picked on by Bill O'Reilly and other men just like him," shouted Tantaros, loud enough for all around the ring to hear. "They try to take advantage of us, when all we ever wanted was a fair chance. And this lying sack of deceit is in denial about what he clearly knows he did to each of us."

The crowd exploded with cheers and whistles.

What was supposed to be a battle between two former titans of cable news talk, turned into an exhibition of sisterhood standing up against the evil that possesses some men. As the smiling women stood with arms raised at center-ring, the music came back on over the speakers throughout the stadium. Only this time, it wasn't the theme from *Rocky*, but Katy Perry's song, *Roar*, blaring throughout Yankee Stadium, as the proud women at center ring and across the stadium danced, pumping their right fists in the air, letting the world know that all women and girls deserve to be treated with respect.

CHAPTER 11

AND NOW, THE AWARD FOR "MOST OUTRAGED NEWS COMMENTATOR"

On Thursday, October 5th, 2017, an unusually hot and sunny Fall day in New York City, a thousand television news and media executives along with news and documentary producers and journalists entered Lincoln Center, eager to find out if they would receive an Emmy Award in one of the fifty categories honoring exemplary journalism.

Longtime and highly respected newsman, Charles Osgood, would be honored on this evening at the *38th Annual News and Documentary Emmy Award Presentation* in the Frederick P. Rose Hall, where every seat in the auditorium was filled with anxious news professionals, hoping to walk away with a golden statue recognizing their work in 2016.

As the industry presenters announced award winner after award winner, PBS was wearing out the carpet leading up to the stage, winning twelve awards, with CBS right behind them with nine. But it was the new award category that had been added to this year's event which many were very eager to witness.

All eyes were on the stage as the presenter for the coveted award was announced, "Ladies and gentlemen, please welcome Mr. Michael Richards."

Surprise filled the hall when one of the stars from the television program *Seinfeld,* dressed in a black tuxedo, entered the stage from the wings. This was not someone who normally would be involved with the News Emmy Award presentations, but, as the professionals in their seats quickly agreed in half-whispered discussions, it made sense for this award.

Richards, flashed his always hilarious, Kramer-character's big smile and pointed at several people he recognized in the audience as he walked with his familiar and humorous Kramer-like stride to the podium.

"Well, I'm really upset now!" erupted Richards, in that loud high-pitched voice, so familiar to *Seinfeld* fans. "Really upset! But I guess I'm just going to have to read the nominees anyway!"

Nearly everyone in the audience busted out laughing, apparently they were all *Seinfeld* fans who knew Richards's character and the hilarity of the inflection in his voice when he gets upset. Richards just smiled at the wonderful reception he was receiving. Then in his normal voice read, "I have been asked to present this new award for *Most Outraged News Commentator.*

"Wait I need to say that again." Then he went back into his loud, crazy, high-pitched Kramer voice and said, "For the *Most Outraged New Commentator*!" He paused. "Hey, I ought to win this."

Laughter swept across the large auditorium. News executives sitting in the balcony looked on with great anticipation, knowing that if their host won the award, it would generate higher ratings, resulting in more ad dollars for the network and a bigger bonus for them. They knew people love to watch 'outraged' commentators and this was the first year it would be honored at this prestigious journalism awards show.

"And the nominees are," he continued. "From MSNBC's *Morning Joe*, Mika Brzezinski."

A video clip came up on the large screen to the right of Richards.

"How dare he call me low I.Q. Crazy Mika!" an outraged Brzezinski said, in response to Republican candidate Donald Trump's attacks on her, as a bit of froth emanated from her mouth. "He says I'm bleeding bad from a face-lift! He's such a low-life. Here, Mr. Trump. Here's a box of Cheerios, perfect for you and your teensy hands."

The box read, "Made for Little Hands." The screen froze on that shot as the audience applauded Brzezinski's nomination and the large screen showed her in the audience holding up that box of Cheerios.

"Very nice," said Richards.

One of the network executives from MSNBC, smiling wide, pointed toward the screen and said, "That was some excellent frothing. Our liberal audience loves her for that."

Richards continued, "Our second nominee is Gloria Borger from CNN."

The video clip showed Borger on the panel at CNN in a heated discussion with Wolf Blitzer.

"You are only as good as your sources, and when one source tells me one thing about Trump and another source tells me something completely different, well then I don't know what to believe!" Borger said, her eyes growing wider, voice louder, and a river of white froth pouring from her mouth. "I just don't know what to believe about Trump! Or who is telling the truth! You're right, Wolf, you grey-bearded twit! I need better sources."

The screen froze with the shot of Borger, zooming in on her white-frothed mouth and the crazed look on her face. Then the screen changed to show her in the audience with a towel wiping her face and smiling at her overzealous commentary style.

"Excellent frothing, Gloria," said Richards, looking out at Borger.

The network executive from CNN looked over at the now-jealous MSNBC exec who thought Brzezinski's frothing was good enough to win, and said, "Now that's some serious crazed frothing, eh?"

Richards looked at the monitor in front of him and said, "The third nominee is Rush Limbaugh from the Excellence in Broadcasting Network."

The screen showed a photo of the grey-haired Limbaugh wearing a blue dress-shirt sitting in his radio studio and talking into an EIB microphone, as the audio recording of his show played over the sound system in the auditorium. It sounded like he was shouting at the top of his lungs, but as his long-time listeners would attest, that was his normal outraged voice level on the program.

"These drive-by media are just looking for anything to pin on Trump to delegitimize his election and get him out of the White House," shouted Limbaugh. "The liberals just can't get over the fact that he won the election! They just won't accept it!"

The camera returned to Richards clapping. Limbaugh apparently hadn't shown up at the event which has been deemed too liberally biased, resulting in FOX News boycotting it and requesting not to be included in the nominations. Nonetheless, this was a category where Limbaugh's outrage could not be denied and he did not prohibit it.

"MSNBC's Chris Matthews," Richards said introducing the fourth nominee and a video appeared on the large screen of Matthews on his weekday show *Hardball* interviewing Kellyanne Conway, who was Donald Trump's Presidential campaign manager at that time.

"What did you think back in March when I interviewed your candidate and he said women should be punished for having abortions," asked Matthews with spittle flying out of his mouth so far it even reached the camera lens.

When Conway tried to answer, Matthews cut her off saying, "What did you think when he got in that fight with Megyn Kelly?"

Conway leaned in and Matthews cut her off again, "Now, I don't think anyone's an innocent here. We're all combatants. We're all in the field. We're all good guys and bad guys. But what did you think when you heard his comments?"

Again Conway tried to answer, but again was cut off by the wild-eyed MSNBC journalist with saliva all over his mouth and chin, saying, "Did you think this guy's got to get an education or what? He needs to be taught some things, don't you think?"

Conway had a blank stare on her face not knowing if she would be able to answer and that was the shot frozen on the screen as the camera moved back to Richards, who looked out at Matthews in the audience and said, "Pretty worked up there, eh Chris?"

The Irish-American from Pennsylvania, Matthews, just laughed.

"And our final nominee, also from MSNBC, Rachel Maddow," Richards said.

The clip came up with Maddow, wearing a black jacket over a black top, looking directly into the camera with arms flailing to make her point, saying, "South Carolina leans Republican now, but it's thin. Kansas leans Republican, but thin. And if Donald Trump has the best day of his life on election day and wins all of the toss up states, which would be insane because no one wins all of the toss-up states, he would still lose."

The clip then cut to election night and Rachel Maddow looking into the camera, wearing the same black jacket and top, breathed a large sigh of frustration and said, "You're awake by the way. You're not having a terrible, terrible dream. Also, you're not dead and you haven't gone to hell. This is your life now. This is our election. This is our country. It's real!"

Then the video transitioned to the next day and Maddow was actually crying on the air saying, "Bad stuff happens. Even sometimes potential end of the world stuff. Sometimes it happens to be your generation, your workplace, your country."

The frame froze there as the camera showed Maddow in the audience wearing the same black jacket and top, forcing the best smile she could exhibit under such embarrassing circumstances.

"I don't think she should have been nominated for this award," said the MSNBC executive to his CNN pal. "She was upset, not outraged. No frothing! Just upset."

"I agree," said Mr. CNN. "Should have been Ashleigh Banfield. She can really speak out strongly against all that's wrong in the world."

"Sure, but can she froth?" asked Mr. MSNBC.

"No, that's why we sent her over to HLN to work on that. Gloria is coaching her."

Richards, back on stage, clapped, then said, "There were two other nominees. Ann Coulter was strongly considered for this award, but none of our producers had the courage to contact her for fear of being yelled at. And Norah O'Donnell had to be disqualified when it was learned that the frothing she exhibited was actually produced by an Alka-Seltzer tablet in her mouth. Fake froth!"

Upon hearing this news, the CBS Network executive in the balcony quickly typed a note into his iPhone. *Next time, try Fluff marshmallow crème.*

"Norah never struck me as much of a frother anyway, so it's probably better," laughed Richards as he opened the envelope, "And the winner for *Most Outraged News Commentator* goes to.... Oh my. Well, I'm feeling a little like Warren Beatty here. Can I have the organizers come out to help me? Is there anyone here from Yangaroo?"

The audience laughed thinking Richards was making a joke.

"No, that's actually who manages this event," explained the *Seinfeld* star. "Yangaroo! Hah!"

Just then a representative from Yangaroo hopped up on the stage to Richards, looked at the paper with the winner listed and nodded.

"Well, okay then, I guess this is correct," continued Richards. "We have a tie and the winners are Mika Brzezinski and Rush Limbaugh."

With Limbaugh a no-show at the liberal-dominated event, the camera showed Brzezinski dressed in a very lovely, white, mid-length dress and matching high heels, highlighted by her short, beautiful blonde hair. She seemed a bit embarrassed to receive this new award. She turned to her fiancé, Joe Scarborough, and received a congratulatory kiss, then walked toward the stage.

Richards handed her a shining golden Emmy statue and respectfully shook her hand to congratulate her. She stepped to the podium and looked out at her fellow news contemporaries, saying, "I believe that I represent the common person out there, the average Joe and Josephine who are beside themselves over Donald Trump as our President. He is not a good man. He's a liar. He's a greedy, self-centered misogynist. And he has very small hands!"

The entire audience erupted with laughter and applause.

"Yes, teensy! He needs to be on that box of Cheerios. And when I go a little woohoo on the air, I believe that I am just mirroring millions of our viewers at home who are also going a little woohoo about the times we are now living in, thanks to the Moron in Chief. And yes, I do believe that's exactly how Rex Tillerson, Steve Bannon, and everyone else who knows Trump, refers to him.

"So, this is not a normal award in journalism, but I think it highlights the fact that news and reporting has changed in America. And maybe it's for the better, maybe not. So, I would like to thank everyone who helped me win this statue for being so outraged about the small handed one, including my lawyer, my publicist, my accountant, my stylist...."

The orchestra began to play letting the *Morning Joe* co-star know that it was time to get off the stage. She tried to continue to thank her fiancé, but they played louder drowning her out. She smiled, waved to the audience and gracefully exited the stage holding her golden statue.

"Well that brings us to the end of the awards ceremony tonight," said a very happy Michael Richards, having successfully completed his duties. "Thanks for coming and goodnight."

As all the professionals from the news business exited the Lincoln Center, a young staff of volunteers handed them each a complimentary box of Cheerios, a new box with Mika Brzezinski holding the Emmy statuette on the front. Apparently, Cheerios was the main sponsor of the awards event and knew she would win. Under her photo was written:

<u>Most Outraged News Commentator!</u>
<u>Mika Brzezinski</u>

After this event, it was reported that President Trump banned Cheerios from the White House saying, "I'm a bacon, eggs, and corn flakes guy. I love the Kellogg's corn flakes. They're great! They should put me on the box and state that the cornflakes are 'Made for Large Hands.' Very Large! Believe me! There's no problem there. Believe me."

CHAPTER 12

WHY DAVID LETTERMAN WENT TO NETFLIX

A white-bearded, always professionally-dressed David Letterman in blue suit and tie, sat with legs crossed, revealing beige socks, on a semi-lit stage in a New York City theater filled with audience members watching him interview the former President of the United States, Barack Obama, who was sitting across from him in a comfortable brown leather armchair.

"Two wars and a collapsing economy, welcome to the gig," Letterman said to the smiling Obama, recalling the state of the union when the first black President of the United States entered the White House in January of 2009. "Where's the handbook on that?"

"I think people forget how bad things were back then," said Obama, wearing a black suit with an open-collared white dress shirt, sitting upright with left hand resting on his crossed legs, exposing his matching black socks and shined shoes. "As it turns out, the economy was collapsing faster than it did during the Great Depression. The month I took office, we lost eight hundred thousand jobs just in that month. And one of the things I'm proudest of is that within a year, we actually had the economy growing again."

This was a serious interview about serious subjects between two serious men, both of whom possess a terrific sense of humor, which was injected into the discussion when appropriate. But Letterman wasn't there to get laughs. This is where he wanted to be in 2018. He was doing work he could enjoy, spending his time doing interviews that he believed were important.

This was a long way from the Comedy Store on Sunset Boulevard in Los Angeles where Letterman got his standup comedy start in the mid-1970s, before moving to New York to launch a new NBC late night comedy talk show on February 1, 1982, called *Late Night with David Letterman.* His show aired at 12:30 a.m., following *The Tonight Show with Johnny Carson.* Ten years later, when the legendary Carson, the undisputed King of Late Night, was unceremoniously pushed out the door at NBC by network executives, most thought Letterman would be the heir-apparent, including Carson, whose final show aired on May 22, 1992. It didn't work out that way however, as those same brilliant NBC execs ordained Jay Leno as the new host.

Letterman, who often referred to those NBC executives as weasels, decided to move over to CBS and start his own late-night show. On August 30, 1993, *The Late Show with David Letterman* first aired, competing directly with Leno in the 11:30 p.m. timeslot. As great as Letterman was on *Late*

Night, he took his comedy talents to a much higher level on *CBS*. His final show was broadcast on May 20, 2015, ending a thirty-three-year successful run of hosting late-night comedy talk shows on national television in America.

The year prior to his retirement however, has been a subject of many rumors and speculation. Supposedly, there were indications that Letterman had reached a point in his life and career where he wanted to do things a little differently. The rumors were supposedly born of a show taped on Monday, August 11, 2014. Apparently, something incredible had taken place on that show which CBS kept away from the general public. There were several "Fake News" stories published, but there was never an eyewitness account. Only those who were in the audience, or working on the show that afternoon of the taping, knew the real story.

And now, for the first time, two honest and courageous audience members who witnessed the events that took place in the Ed Sullivan Theater that afternoon, have now approached this highly reputable publication, *The Real News!* These eyewitnesses agreed to come forward with this untold story as long as their names were kept anonymous. So, we made that deal with Willie Washington and Freddy Cronkite, both distant relatives of two of the most famous honest men in American history. So, as promised, we will keep their names anonymous. Audience members A and B were seated in the second row of the famed Broadway theater for the taping of the show. So, for the first time ever, here is the detailed written account, which has been notarized, plasticized, and sent in the mail, so it is official and can't be destroyed.

EXCLUSIVE REPORT!!!

It was a hot sunny summer day in New York and David Letterman sat at his desk listening to reality television star and actress Paris Hilton tell her story about walking out in her garden and noticing that something had changed.

"I don't know how it happened, but when I walked over to my citronella bush, which I had just planted," she said with a look of great concern across her face. "David, the bush was only thirty inches long and I counted one hundred and seventy-three leaves, which meant it hadn't been growing much. David, it just didn't look right when I brushed my hand across it. It didn't seem to have much life to it. Do you understand, David, not much life!"

"Yes, I understand, not much life," he responded, wondering what in the world this celebrity actress was talking about and whether she would be changing the subject soon before all the viewers changed the channel to watch Jimmy Fallon, the new host of *The Tonight Show*.

"Then I stood back and wondered," Hilton continued. "David, I wondered how I would bring my citronella bush back to its healthy state. Do you know what I mean, David?"

Letterman looked like he was fighting himself to try and pay attention to another completely boring story from a movie actress, booked merely because she was an actress in a new release from one of the major studios. This kind of interview seemed to happen all too often and Letterman sat there wondering to himself why he continued putting himself through that type of torture. It was his show. Couldn't he just do what he wanted to do in terms of booking guests? He had wisely established a format to use the first half the show for the comedy he wanted to perform, which usually meant that was the best part of the show. And if viewers knew the guests were duds, they could just turn off their television and go to sleep. Letterman knew that of his five weekly tapings, ten guests per week, he would probably have to endure ramblings from two of those guests, who were absolutely hopeless and would bore him to tears. For more than thirty-two years, he put up with that calculation, realizing it usually totaled about six minutes a week that he would have to endure. He also knew that no matter what he thought of those guests, there were people in America who sat and listened to every word of the celebrity tripe as if it were Franklin Delano Roosevelt giving his great, "The only thing we have to fear" speech.

It's all about the ratings in TV land, and Letterman was a pro who knew if he didn't regularly beat Jimmy Fallon and Jimmy Kimmel on ABC, he would be canceled or replaced. So, he continued to keep booking inane, mundane movie stars, too many of whom couldn't deliver an interesting line unless it had been written for them by a talented screenwriter and directed by a Hollywood professional.

These new celebrity stars added to their fame promoting their movies on publicity tours going from *The Today Show* to *Good Morning America*, sometimes *CBS This Morning,* and then onto *The View.* If they were smart enough and big enough, they might receive a booking on *The Daily Show with Jon Stewart* and perhaps the *Colbert Report.* But the icing on the cake, the show that truly earned them greater celebrity, was an appearance on *The Late Show with David Letterman.*

They all wanted to be on Letterman, the Johnny Carson of his time. And although some celebrities were intimidated by the talk show giant, due to perceptions that evolved from interviews that didn't go so well with pop singing star Madonna, or the sometimes-combative singer Cher, the vast majority still wanted to be sitting in that seat next to David. Even in his sixties, in the new millennium, Letterman still had THE show to be booked on in New York. It was status in Hollywood and that's what counted.

"Yes, I know exactly what you mean," said Letterman to Paris Hilton, whom he knew would be part of that six minutes he would endure each week. Nonetheless, a professional, he forced a smile with all the energy he could draw from his limp body, made sick by the incredibly boring story being delivered by this young actress. "Yes, the citronella bush," Letterman stammered. "You had to bring it back to health."

The actress could hear in David's voice that he was fascinated by the story and continued, "Not only that, David, but there were grub worms moving all about the garden and I just stood there and watched them move all about."

"Grub worms?" said Letterman, realizing there was no hope.

"And believe me David when I tell you this, please," she said raising her hands up in an animated pose because of the importance of this new information. "The grub worms crawled to the left and then for no reason at all, turned and started crawling to the right. Can you believe that, David?"

"You are kidding?" asked the long-time talk show giant, looking around his desk for a bottle of Extra Strength Tylenol.

"No, I wouldn't make that up," she said.

"Couldn't make it up," agreed David, who rolled his eyes and moved his chair to the center of his desk, putting his head between his two hands with his elbows resting on the desktop.

"Are you okay David?" she asked with great concern. "Have I frightened you with this story of the grubs and the citronella bush?"

Letterman then lifted his hands over his ears and looked over at his producer, Barbara Gaines, who couldn't understand what he was doing or if something was wrong with him. Was he having another heart attack?

He took his hands off his ears, snapped back up and turned toward the actress, again trying to smile. "So, the citronella was attacked by the grub worms?"

The actress beamed realizing her story had made an impact with the host and he couldn't wait to hear more about it.

"Yes, David," she said. "And that's not the best part of the story."

"It gets better? Thank you, Lord!" he said wishing a praying mantis would show up to eat the grub worms, the citronella bush, and hopefully the actress.

"Yes, because you see somehow when the grub was moving through the soil, some of the black dirt shot up onto the cement next to the garden," she laughed, slapping her right hand against her thigh, which was completely exposed by the very short skirt she was wearing. "David, are you hearing me? Some of the black dirt was now on the white cement."

As the camera showed Letterman, he was clearly biting his lip as he stared with a blank look on his face at this moron in front of him, boring the crap out of him, as well as his studio audience and the television viewing audience across the country.

"I stood straight up and looked at it and thought, wow, that black dirt is now on the white cement!"

That's when David Letterman stood up from his chair and went ballistic, "Stop! Stop! Please stop! I can't take it anymore. I can't do this anymore.

"Do you have any idea how much you are boring me and every other American watching this show tonight, although my guess is most have changed the channel, fallen asleep, or killed themselves listening to this incredibly stupid story."

Paris Hilton looked at him in dismay, "David, is this one of your gags? Am I part of one of your comedy bits now?" she asked, smiling and shaking her head like she was in on his joke.

"No, you are the comedy bit!" he said, killing her smile and head-shaking antics. "Look, I can put up with Madonna coming here to push a children's book which she claims to have written but doesn't know anything about what's actually in the book. Or Cher calling me names. Or Joaquin Phoenix coming in here pretending to be someone else and trying to make me believe it. But I can't take another stupid story from a movie actor or actress who thinks it's so fascinating because they have been elevated in the public spotlight due to their good looks and ability to read and deliver lines on a script. I just can't do it anymore!

"Ms. Hilton, I know you are now a big celebrity with millions of adoring fans who love to watch your work, but I am no longer the right guy to be sitting here listening to this drivel, which you seem to think is so fascinating.

"I apologize if I am upsetting you with this, but we need to end this interview now and you need to leave. I am going to reformat this show if it's the last thing I do in this world."

The beautiful blonde actress in the low-cut pink blouse and matching short skirt just looked around the stage for her manager, her agent, the show's producer, the FBI, CIA, President of the United States, anyone who could explain to her what was happening. After all, she was Paris Hilton, the star of popular movies and a TV reality show who all of the paparazzi followed across the world. She was voted one of the most beautiful celebrities in the world by *People Magazine*, dated whomever she liked whenever she liked, and made more than ten million dollars the previous year. She was not someone to be dismissed by a talk show host because he didn't appreciate the amazing adventures of the citronella bush and grub worm which she so skillfully recited to an audience eager to hear her tale.

Seeing this unexpected event, *The Late Show*'s executive producer Barbara Gaines quickly told the director in the booth to stop the taping, then took off her headset and walked over to her star to discuss the problem, and pointed to the band leader, Paul Shaffer, to start playing some music.

"Wooly Bully," Paul said to his band, choosing the upbeat *Sam the Sham* song he hoped would quickly change the mood in the auditorium. "One, two, three," he counted off and with great energy the popular bald-headed band-leader began playing his keyboard.

The thin, pale-faced announcer with a striking head of red hair, Alan Kalter, knew the drill and walked to the front of the studio audience with microphone in hand, "Is everyone having a great time?" he asked, not having any idea himself what had just transpired. The lights of the studio were turned on clearly indicating the taping had stopped.

"How many have waited several months to get their tickets to *The Late Show*?" he asked and watched the hands of most in the audience go up. "Well, I am here to tell you how lucky you are to be part of an audience that is watching some television history. Please don't be alarmed by what you have just witnessed, because it's all part of an elaborate comedy bit we have been rehearsing for weeks."

Many in the audience looked relieved to hear this news and began to laugh, realizing they had watched a very funny comedy bit performed by their favorite talk show host and a very popular actress.

"Because remember folks," continued Kalter, who had made a mental note to visit St. Patrick's Cathedral the next morning for confession. "I'm TV's Uncle Jerry or you can just call me Big Red!"

A burst of laugher erupted from the audience, filling the famed Ed Sullivan Theater, followed by loud applause. Once again, everything was fine and dandy at *The Late Show* that Monday afternoon. Everyone was enjoying themselves. Why shouldn't they be? It was all a gag.

But why was Paris Hilton standing and yelling at the gray-suited executive? Was she upset that Letterman had blown the lines of the comedy bit? Maybe she didn't like the way she looked in the sketch? And why did Letterman look so distraught, constantly placing his hand on his head as if he was suffering a migraine headache, as he talked with his long-time producer and friend, Barbara Gaines? Either way, everyone in the audience looked happy, but continued watching the action on the stage as the incredibly talented Shaffer and his band played and sang in unison, "Wooly bully, Wooly bully!"

Paris Hilton and the executive walked off the stage together into the wings, Hilton still looking livid, continuing her rampage toward the man. The four cameras on the stage were pulled back to the side by their operators and Barbara Gaines stepped to the side as Letterman walked toward his announcer, who handed him the microphone, then motioned toward Shaffer to stop the music.

"Hello folks," said Letterman, looking and sounding business-like, not his normal tone to his audience. "I would personally like to apologize to you for what has transpired here this afternoon."

Many in the audience looked around wondering if the comedy bit had continued and if they were now actually stars in it. They looked for hidden cameras.

"I have been doing this show at *CBS* for more than twenty-one years and have really felt blessed to be able to do what I love," he sincerely explained to a large group of people who were well aware of Dave's career. "But there comes a time when one realizes it's time to make some changes and that's what you witnessed here today. We are going to finish the show today as planned, but we will be changing the format. The point is that you are part of the last studio audience to see the final show of the long-running format that will end today. And because of this, we will offer each of you an opportunity to come back and see the new show when we kick it off in about a month from today, we hope. Thanks for your patience and understanding and for supporting our show."

At first, the audience looked a little shocked, but within a minute, as Letterman walked back to his desk, they began to rise and clap their hands, which built to a loud applause, cheering, whistling and then a chant of, "DA-VID! DA-VID! DA-VID!"

As Letterman reached his desk and turned to see this wonderful reaction, he just smiled. Barbara Gaines put her headset back on, the lights over the studio audience were turned back down, the four cameras rolled back out, the makeup lady checked David's face and within a few minutes, the show was starting again.

"Ladies and gentlemen, Brian Regan," said Letterman, introducing the last guest of the old format, who fortunately was one of the funniest standup comedians in the world. For the next four minutes, Regan performed his very popular bit about driving himself to the emergency room, supported by his incredible gift for physical humor, especially his hilarious facial expressions.

Letterman sat enjoying the comedy of the hilarious Mr. Regan, which was also killing the audience. This comedian didn't need applause signs lit to get the audience to laugh or clap. They loved him and so did Letterman, realizing his days of listening to mundane citronella bush and grub stories had come to an end, thank God!

When the show aired later that evening, the producers edited out Letterman going ballistic. For Hilton's portion, they found a sentence from the actress's interview that they could legitimately end the segment on, cutting it after Hilton's revelation that, "Wow, that black dirt is on the cement." The producers added canned laughter and applause to follow that line, as if that were actually funny. They contacted Hilton's publicist to let her know they had made the edit and her client looked perfectly fine.

"I will have Mr. Letterman know that Paris told that same story on four other shows before going on *The Late Show* and they all loved it!" Hilton's publicist said to the *The Late Show* public relations director. "Savannah Guthrie and Kelly Ripa both loved the grub worm story. The BLACK dirt was on the white cement, you know?" the publicist emphasized, wondering how anyone could miss the humor of such a great comedy story. As it turned out, Hilton's people decided to let it go, but word leaked from *CBS* staffers and, within a week, news and entertainment bloggers had picked up on it. The sources attributed were anonymous.

Letterman's public relations department worked to squelch any news about an incident during the taping of the show, calling a press conference the next day to announce a potential format change for *The Late Show*.

"We would like to maintain a freshness to the show, a new format utilizing our greatest talents and the segments that have worked for us in the past," said Barbara Gaines in front of a packed press conference held in a third-floor conference room at the Marriott Marquis in Times Square.

A reporter raised his hand, "Does that mean no more movie stars promoting their films any longer?" asked a veteran entertainment reporter from *The New York Times*.

"Unless they can juggle, knock a pizza off the top of a Christmas tree with a football, run and jump over a taxi, or skateboard off a ramp and over a moving truck, it's not likely they will be booked," said Gaines, smiling and hopeful that *CBS* would allow them the opportunity to improve the show.

The press conference helped give *The Late Show* staff some time to discuss reformatting the show with *CBS* executives before the bloggers did their damage and the controversy hit the proverbial fan. The mainstream media picked up on the story and Paris Hilton was being credited for this potential new format change to late night television. This earned her tremendous publicity and offers to star in two new movies. In a personal meeting with two producers from TriStar Pictures, she accepted them both, but insisted on a third project to star in about the plight of the grub worm trapped in a world of unhealthy citronella bushes. The two producers quickly checked her very high Q-rating and box office receipts from her last film, then told her how much they loved the idea.

"Pure genius!" said one producer. "The black dirt on the white cement. Really funny!"

Media critics and bloggers demanded to see the tape of the controversial moment, but *The Late Show* lawyers knew that would mean a lawsuit from Hilton's camp. Unlike President Richard Nixon's staff, *The Late Show* managers actually burned the tapes in question and within a few months, the story ended. Well, the real story ended, but that only led to conspiracy theorists taking that ball and running just as far as they could with it.

A year later, Oliver Stone released his newest film, *The Lost Late Show Tapes*, which alleged that there was no incident between Hilton and Letterman, as was the popular myth being supported by the mainstream media, who were obviously in the pocket of the network. No, Stone presented his theory that both John F. Kennedy and Elvis appeared on *The Late Show* to let the world know that they had been alive all of these years. However, during the interview, Jimmy Hoffa came running in from the wings with a snub-nosed .38 pistol and killed both Kennedy and Elvis at point-blank range. He then ran down the main aisle of the theater and just as he reached the auditorium doors, bumped into a heavyset Lance Armstrong on his bike, who wrestled Hoffa to the ground. But Hoffa shot him too, then stood up and warned everyone in the theater that if they ever told anyone about this, he would find all of them and kill them. Then he jumped on Armstrong's bike and rode out the back door never to be seen again.

According to Stone, that's why *The Late Show* producers decided to burn the tapes. There was absolutely nothing to support Stone's theory, however his film finished second in box office receipts the weekend it was released and Stone received Academy Award nominations for Best Original Screenplay and Best Director. To promote those awards, he was booked on Jimmy Kimmel's show. Interestingly enough, the other guests booked on the show that evening were Paris Hilton, Madonna, and Cher.

CBS shot down Gaines's proposal to reformat the show and shortly afterwards, David Letterman announced he would retire. When he left The Ed Sullivan Theater for the last time on that Wednesday in May of 2015, he walked out the door with Gaines and said, "Someday, I'm going to do another talk show and interview people who have something important to say."

Gaines just laughed and said, "Oh yeah, like who, Barack Obama?"

CHAPTER 13

HARDBALL GRABS CONGRESS BY THE LUG-NUTS

On a cold and rainy Friday night in April of 2018, after an exhaustive week hosting his national cable news program, *Hardball*, a worn down, stressed out Chris Matthews entered his Nantucket vacation home where his wife, Kathleen, was waiting for him with dinner on the table. Matthews was glad to be there. Five straight days of reporting on President Donald Trump, his potential meeting with North Korea's leader Kim Jong Un, Robert Mueller's on-going investigation into alleged Russian collusion with the Trump campaign, and the never-ending border wall debate, left *Hardball's* host worn out and frustrated. Matthews felt like nothing he said to the 1.6 million viewers of his MSNBC show had helped. However, he knew his national cable network was enjoying a growing audience since Trump took office, so it was all good.

Matthews, a highly intelligent, energetic, though somewhat polarizing, news talk show host launched his program in 1997 and has enjoyed great success. His career evolved from congressional aide to speechwriter to newspaper columnist to national news talk show host. His compensation as a print journalist could never touch his new-found fame and fortune on television. Unlike so many in the television news business, Matthews's career roots and experiences kept his perspective real, not allowing his ego to take control of his words and actions. Even with his wealth and fame, he could still see the truth in the world; at least his version of the truth. His honesty and perspective drew viewers to *Hardball*, mostly liberal Democrats, but also many independents and even some Republicans.

Matthews loved politics, seemingly spending every waking hour talking, thinking, and reading about current politics or history and biographies as fast as publishers could churn them out. He loved it so much that he authored several books about political history, lending his opinions and insight on the science that determines the course of our nation. Matthews's recall of historical names, places, and events was astounding. His knowledge, brains, and rapid-fire questioning of guests, with no regard for their position or status, made him a newsman to watch each evening across America.

Whereas many Americans are turned off by what might be termed as Matthews's "rude" or "interruptive" approach during interviews, enough viewers seem to appreciate the fact that he won't allow his subjects to tap dance or spin their way out of a question. He cuts them off mid-spin, mid-dance. He plays hardball.

Since the show's debut, Matthews had tried to maintain a neutral position on politics, never really voicing his opinions on issues and whether he was left, right, or up the middle. However, that changed quite a bit around 2009 when he let America know that he was the same Democrat that worked as a speechwriter for former U.S. President, Jimmy Carter, and spent time as a top aide to the leader of the House of Representatives, Tip O'Neill.

Perhaps that was weighing on his mind on this rainy Friday, as he sat at the kitchen table of his cozy vacation hideaway eating clam chowder with his lovely successful wife, Kathleen. Perhaps he knew the time had come for him to make a decision on his future. Since he was a boy, his dream had been to become a member of the U.S. Senate. And with mid-term elections coming up in November, he had reached a crossroads in his life where he actually considered leaving his high-paying, highly-visible television job to pursue his childhood dream—to become a senator from the great state of Pennsylvania. So, the time had come for him to face the question of his life: Should he run for the Senate against Bob Casey, giving the Democrats a better chance to defeat Trump-backed Republican, Representative Lou Barletta?

But could anyone imagine what the Senate would be like if Matthews did run, win, and join the ranks of the elite 100?

❧

It was Thursday, January 3, 2019. This was not just any other Thursday for the seventy-three-year-old Chris Matthews as he prepared for his first session of Congress. The 100 elite American senators were milling about the cloak room area and lobby, preparing for a debate on a bailout for the American lug-nut industry. The big business bailouts had begun during the end of President George W. Bush's administration and continued into President Barack Obama's time in office. But now, there was a new Commander in Chief, President Trump, and he strongly favored big business, which seemed incredibly unfair to Matthews.

There were so many contentious issues being fought between Congress and the White House that those with an interest in the lug-nut industry thought they could just sneak a bailout into the new budget to help those who funded their respective campaigns; which was all that really mattered to them.

Three U.S. senators, one with his state's lug-nut revenue on the line, stood at the door awaiting the new junior senator from Pennsylvania, who entered the historic assembly with a skip in his stride and energy in his demeanor that predicted a new enthusiasm and attitude on the Senate floor.

New York's Chuck Schumer, Michigan's Gary Peters, and Ohio's Rob Portman waited for Matthews outside the Senate doors, to stop him before he reached the legendary chamber. "Senator Matthews!" announced the sixty-year-old Peters, a financial expert who won his Senate campaign after long-serving Senator Carl Levin retired. "Let us be the first to welcome you to the Senate."

The tall, blonde-haired, newly-elected senator from Pennsylvania smirked, shaking the hand of each of the three veterans. "Thank you. This is a very exciting day for me. I have waited for this my entire life. Public service—greatest thing an American can do," said Matthews, who spent two years in the Peace Corps after graduating from Holy Cross College.

"Chris, I know you are well-versed in what goes on down here, but I hope you will follow our lead today on this important legislation," said Senator Portman, who won his Ohio Senate seat in 2011. "I know you have covered this group for years, but it's a little different once you become a member of this exclusive club."

"I'm honored," Matthews said. "And appreciate your support."

"As Democrats, we have a duty to represent our constituents," said the now famous Senate Minority Leader from New York, Senator Chuck Schumer. "You know that, but we have to really stick together sometimes if we are to be successful, especially as Democrats, right Chris? That's the key to most of these debates and battles. A few dissenters can ruin it for the rest of us."

"I know what you are saying," Matthews replied, then reminded the senators of his experience with other political leaders. "Remember I worked closely with Tip O'Neill and President Carter."

"Today is going to be a test," said Peters of Michigan, who had the most at stake with one of his biggest constituencies at the forefront of the debate. "This bill is important for so many businesses that depend on the lug-nut industry. We have to get behind them, make it happen."

"Really?" asked Matthews, somewhat puzzled by the obvious agenda being sold to him.

"Absolutely, Americans are holding rallies throughout the country calling for support of the industry," said Peters, showing him the headline on the front page of *The New York Times*.

"Michigan nuts for Lug-nuts!" read Matthews, smirking at the headline.

"Chris, we need you and every other Democratic senator to vote for this, if we are to be successful," Peters emphasized. "Because I promise you, the Republicans have no interest in voting for lug-nuts."

"You know President Trump will support this bill," Matthews interjected.

Portman cut him off. "Yes, but he'll use it as a bargaining chip for something else, like the twenty billion dollars he needs to build that damn wall!"

The four senators proceeded through the door and down the famous blue carpet that led to each of their desks. Matthews's appearance drew the attention of every senator in the chamber, watching the man many had worked to befriend over the past decade, hoping it would pay off with an appearance on *Hardball.* Matthews walked to his Senate desk in the back row, second from the left. This was the same desk two of his heroes had occupied, Senator John F. Kennedy, taking his seat in 1953, followed by his brother, Senator Edward M. Kennedy in 1962. There was a great deal of history and courage that had taken place at that desk. Matthews walked behind it and just stood there running his right hand across the top, hoping he could live up to his predecessors.

The senate majority leader from Kentucky, Mitch McConnell, walked behind the rostrum, picked up the wooden gavel, and pounded it three times to start the session. The first order of business was to swear in the new members of the Senate. The Vice President, Mike Pence, was introduced to rousing cheers from the left side of the chamber and made his way to the front with a Bible in his hand. McConnell then called the names of four new senators, asking them to walk to the front of the room where they would be sworn in. Matthews's name was called last and all of the Democratic senators stood and cheered him, roaring their vocal approval that echoed off the walls, leaving the man from Pennsylvania blushing a bit, a reddish hue grew visible on his pale-skinned cheeks. Matthews lifted his right hand up in recognition of the very warm reception he had received.

As the four new senators stood with their right hand raised, repeating the oath of office, Matthews could feel his entire body filled with a tingling sensation that ran right up his spine. It took his focus away from the moment for just a second as he became aware of it. He took it as a sign that he had reached his calling, his true destination in life.

"So help me God," he said, finishing his oath of office, as all of the senators stood to cheer America's new leaders. The four senators waved their appreciation for the reception and walked to their desks, as the formalities came to an end and it was time to get down to business.

From the podium, Senator McConnell introduced the legislation that offered a new bailout plan for the nation's three largest lug-nut makers. It seemed that Congress was still going to use bailouts for struggling businesses a full decade after the Great Recession. As Democratic Senator Peters, followed by Senator Schumer, stood to argue for the new bailout, the Republicans fought mightily against it with Senator Ted Cruz from Texas leading the charge.

"Let the lug-nut people sink or swim on their own," said the man who candidate Trump labeled "Lyin Ted Cruz" during the Presidential race, but later made amends. "Let them make the business adjustments they need to make so they can stay in business, just like any other business in this country. Remember, we bailed out the banks and what did that get us? It got us a host of greedy bankers taking the money and giving themselves bonuses! Bonuses! Is that what we should be doing with the money from honest hard-working Americans? I don't think so!"

That's when the tall, blonde-haired junior senator from Pennsylvania stood. A smile filled the face of Mitch McConnell as he announced, "The chair recognizes the junior senator from Pennsylvania."

It seemed all heads in the assembly turned at once to the back of the room. This would be a moment the entire country would be watching. A man who had become so recognizable to Americans from television news, a celebrity, was now standing in the real political ring. Baseball great Jim Bouton had done it, followed by Ronald Reagan, basketball great Bill Bradley, Al Franken and Sonny Bono. Now it was Matthews's turn, except this celebrity knew the game. He knew it as well as anyone in that room and the senators were aware of it. They knew Matthews's strategy wasn't to "go along" with the crowd. He ran for the Senate with great purpose. He was looking to make an impact, to help his country.

"Thank you, Senator McConnell," he began, and then slowly looked around the room at a sea of senate faces he had come to know, although peripherally through his interviews with them on *Hardball*. "And I would like to maintain the floor, but may I ask questions without giving up the floor?"

That was a highly unusual request, but the Senate leader agreed and the Senate room was soon filled with that oh so familiar voice and speech-pattern. "Things have got to change," said Matthews, pointing his finger at his Democratic colleagues and then addressed the Republican Senator from South Carolina. "Senator Lindsey Graham, let me ask you a question, how can you justify giving lug-nut makers a nickel, a dime, or any help?" A gasp could be heard filling the Senate chamber as three stunned Democratic Senators, Peters, Schumer and Portman, all looked at each other in dismay. What the heck was going on here?

As Graham stood to agree with Matthews, he was quickly cut off.

"I'll tell you how. You can't! You can't justify it. Isn't that right, senator?"

Graham opened his mouth to agree, but was once again cut off.

"There's no point in even answering that question because you know the answer. The lug-nut makers have taken America for a ride for decades and it's time to get off the Merry-Go-Round. It's time to turn this national lug-nut production line in a new direction. Wouldn't you agree, Senator Peters?"

The junior senator from Michigan, who had the most at stake, just chuckled to himself and said, "This country depends on the lug-nut industry...."

Matthews cut him off in mid-sentence, "Depends on them to take the country down with them. Isn't that what you are really trying to say?"

"No," Peters snapped. "Depends on them to keep the economy..."

"Keep it sinking. Keep overpaying for lug-nuts made in this country because we can't get the unions to fall in line and realize things have got to change if the lug-nut industry is to survive in this country. They have to retool and revise the compensation structure. Otherwise they can't compete. Isn't that your point?"

"Not at all," Peters stood, now red-faced and sweating, working very hard to get his point across. "A large majority of the business interests in this country depend on..."

"Depend on the lug-nut makers," Matthews said.

"Right!" Peters shouted.

"And they will go down with them, right?"

"Right! I mean no!" Peters said waving his arms to correct himself.

"So, we are funding a business that can't properly organize itself technically or financially to compete in this century. Is that your point?"

"No!" yelped the frustrated, wide-eyed senator from Michigan.

Schumer and Portman both stood and appealed to majority leader McConnell, who was just as stunned as they were. "Will the junior senator from Pennsylvania concede to a question?"

"Not now, Senator Portman!" said Matthews. "You know I am right, Senator Peters. All of you do! Some of your campaign contributions come from those lug-nut companies. You're more interested in receiving a paycheck under the current system and you don't want that current system to change, do you? No, you like getting those checks. All of you! It keeps you in office. Isn't that what you are really trying to say?"

"No!" said Peters as if on a witness stand in the court of America.

"Of course it is and you would also like to add that if it was up to you, the entire production system would be torn down and rebuilt with more cost-efficient lug-nut making machines, right?"

"Wrong!" Peters snapped.

"And you wouldn't stop there either, would you?"

"Yes, I would. I would stop there. I wouldn't even have gone that far…"

Matthews cut him off, "You would demand new sources of raw materials to make these lug-nuts, wouldn't you?"

"Only if the lug-nut makers could use those materials, moron! I mean Matthews."

"Cow-shit! They can make lug-nuts with cow-shit and iron!" said Matthews, holding up a chart of the new raw materials being tested for lug-nut production.

"Bullshit! You're out of your mind!" the senator fired back.

"Yes, bullshit too! They can make them with bullshit, cow-shit, horseshit, and probably all of the shit coming out of the mouths of some of the senators in this room."

"I object!" demanded Senator Portman. "Would someone remind Mr. Matthews that he is a Democrat?"

"Sit down, this is the U.S. Senate," demanded Matthews. "I have the floor. And I'm an American. We all are. We shouldn't be playing for the Democratic team or Republican team. We should be fighting for what is right for America! For what we know is right, isn't that right, Senator Portman? That's the kind of man you wanted to be growing up in Ohio, learning from the experience of your father, creating the Portman Equipment Company, believing in entrepreneurship, not union lobbyists calling the shots! Isn't that right, Senator Portman?"

"I'm not sure of the question," said Portman, taken aback by the aggressive attack from his fellow Democrat.

"Senator Peters, you won't even consider these ideas, this question, will you? Nor will so many others in this room. Of course not, because that question didn't contribute to any of your campaigns, so you can't even consider that question. So many of you are puppets for your campaign contributors, while pretending to be here representing all of the interests of your state. Isn't that right?"

Peter's face was boiling over as he yelled out, "Not at all! And I am offended by your…"

"By my honesty in identifying what your real purpose is here in this Senate!" Matthews interrupted again.

"No!" sneered an irate Peters, his glasses falling off his nose as he craned his neck and squinted his eyes to watch Matthews continue his tirade.

"Offended by the fact that I'm calling out all of the senators in this room who have lost their way, lost their perspective, taking free trips and other payoffs from multi-million-dollar companies, so they will represent their interests here. Not because those interests are best for America, but because those interests are self-serving to those companies."

"That is ridiculous!" said Senator Schumer, his voice bouncing off the Senate walls.

"Is it ridiculous?" Matthews boomed back, pointing his finger at Senator Schumer. "Or is that too common a theme here in this room? How many good, honest fair-minded senators have quit because of the partisan politics here? How many?"

Schumer opened his mouth to answer, but was cut off.

"Too many! That's how many."

Senator Peters stood and shouted toward the Senate Majority Leader, "I object to this entire presentation!" he appealed to McConnell, as a buzz filled the chamber, many senators amazed at this incredible departure from the normal Senate decorum. The Republicans were grinning from ear to ear with arms folded, while many of Senator Matthews's fellow Democrats stared at him with clenched teeth.

"This is not a courtroom counselor!" directed Matthews to Peters, who was reaching down to pick up his glasses. "I have the floor. So please sit down!"

Senator McConnell interrupted, "I'll give the orders here, Senator Matthews, if you don't mind?"

"I'm sorry, Senator McConnell," Matthews apologized.

"Would you concede the floor to Senator Peters," McConnell appealed, hoping to break this tirade and return the Senate to some level of normalcy.

"I respectfully decline," Matthews informed the Senate leader, continuing.

"I am new to this body, and that is a good thing because like Jimmy Stewart in *Mr. Smith Goes to Washington*, I haven't been corrupted yet. I haven't gotten too comfortable in my Senate seat where sitting in this chair becomes the priority, instead of my privilege to serve the people of my state.

"Public service ladies and gentlemen! Vocation! There are too many in this room who have become too comfortable! You get sent back here because you are voicing the needs of the special interests that fund your campaigns. And they have the money and power to influence so many in your respective states. Isn't that right?"

Senator Schumer rose to his feet and warned, "Watch who you are pointing your finger at Mr. Matthews."

McConnell slammed his gavel, "You don't have the floor Senator Schumer!"

Matthews quickly snapped back at Schumer, "I am pointing my finger at the lug-nut industry today Senator Schumer, which is why I am speaking directly to you, Senator Peters and Senator Portman. But many of you on both sides of the aisle are guilty of the same thing. Big oil, pharmaceutical companies, the insurance industry, Wall Street, bankers! They have had too much to say about how this country is run. And it needs to stop!

"I may only get six years in this seat, but it is one term that I will be proud to serve. I am going to represent the interests of Pennsylvania and voice the interests of the average Joe, the average American who works hard to make ends meet, to provide for his or her family. Sometimes that means making tough decisions, tough choices, like a major re-tooling and restructuring of the lug-nut industry. But that is what is needed. Not a multi-million-dollar bailout to keep the status quo. Who's with me?"

Portman popped up to his feet, "Will the senator from Pennsylvania concede the floor?"

"No sir!" he shouted in the direction of Portman and continued his soliloquy, "Those people in the states that depend on the lug-nut industry aren't going to like this change. They like things the way they are now. But for the long-term, it is in the best interests of all of those people. We just need to retrain them, educate them about the changes and how it will affect their lives. We can't just make the change and hope they understand it. We owe it to them. We need to prepare them."

Matthews stood there for a moment collecting himself, looking at the faces of his colleagues, most of whom looked quite angry. Schumer jumped up, "Will the Senator from Pennsylvania concede the floor?"

"One more statement," said Matthews. "I'm here for the next six years. And I'm not here to make friends. I'm here to help make changes for the good of the citizens of Pennsylvania as well as Americans across the country. If I see wrong-doing, I'll blow the whistle. If I see corruption, I'll put a light on it. If I hear lies spewed in this hallowed hall, I'll call out the liars. And senators, I promise you, the country will know about it. I concede to Senator Schumer."

Before Schumer could speak, everyone seated in the gallery jumped to their feet to applaud Senator Matthews and then began chanting, "Matthews! Matthews!" as Senator McConnell slammed his gavel pleading for "Order! Order!"

A wise guy in the gallery yelled out, "Ham on rye!"

McConnell looked up at the jokester and demanded, "Order, or I will have to clear the gallery!"

Many of the news programs across the country led with Matthews's impromptu speech to the Senate calling him a great American, willing to enter the Senate for the good of all Americans, not just the Democrats. Even one commentator on FOX News, the network which regularly blasted Matthews for some of his biased political commentary while he was the host of *Hardball*, recognized the effort of the new senator from Pennsylvania.

Another FOX commentator, Sean Hannity, who always promotes everything on the right, as being right, was not so kind and concluded, "I think he has just realized the error of his ways all of these years and is looking to join the right side, the conservative Republicans."

Unfortunately, that was the assessment of too many Republicans and Democrats. Senator after senator appeared on the nightly news talk shows and Sunday morning news shows to spin that tale, working to tear down the integrity and legitimacy of Matthews.

"He's only there because people knew him from television," said Senator Peters, who made a point of going on every news show that would have him. "He's a joke! He doesn't belong in the Senate."

It didn't matter to Matthews. He knew the truth and was prepared to stay the course fighting for the good of America. And that's exactly what he did.

❧

With the rain still pouring down onto his Nantucket home that Friday evening in April of 2018, Matthews sat at his kitchen table with his head resting against his right hand, sipping his clam chowder from a spoon while daydreaming of his future. His wife Kathleen's voice brought him out of his political fantasy.

"Chris, when you're finished eating, are we still going into town to look for a new car?" she asked, happy she finally got his attention.

Matthews looked up and smiled. "Yeah, we'll go down there. But I'm only looking at cars that are built with the new cost-efficient lug-nuts. American-made lug-nuts!"

His wife just looked at him, having no idea what he was talking about, and said, "Well, you've got my vote."

CHAPTER 14

THE UNTOLD STORY OF JON STEWART AND STEPHEN COLBERT

Once Donald Trump became President of the United States on January 20, 2017, the host of *The Late Show*, Stephen Colbert, began having a comedy fest with the latest news about the President. It became apparent very quickly that Colbert and his writing staff felt no need to write too many jokes about any other politicians. It was all Trump, all the time; well most of the time anyway. Colbert and company knew all too well that his audience did not like the Trumpster and probably would like to see him thrown into a dumpster or kicked in the family jewels by Eddie Munster. Either way, Colbert's liberal audience would like him to go away as soon as possible.

Colbert's comedy pal, Jon Stewart, made all of that clear in a 2017 interview with Charlie Rose, before the sexual-offender whistle was blown on the CBS morning anchor and

PBS talk show host. At the time of the interview, Rose was still a respected newsman in America, and very directly asked Stewart about Colbert's real feelings toward Trump.

"Does Stephen hate the President as much as it seems he does when he delivers his monologues about him?" asked the curious interviewer.

Stewart just smiled and responded, "If you're asking me if Stephen has any respect for Trump, the answer is no. He thinks he's pure evil, greedy, self-centered, self-absorbed, a bully, and misogynist. How's that? Does that answer your question?"

Rose just chuckled that familiar silent laugh, looking like he hadn't slept in several days. We all learned later that he probably had not slept because he was too busy exposing himself to young women who worked for him.

"Yes, that most certainly answers my question," said Rose. "On a different subject, do you and Stephen ever look back on your time at Comedy Central? And would you say that those were the best years of your lives?"

"We do," said Stewart. "Although you never know what's ahead, right? But that was a time when our comedy ceiling seemed limitless as creative satirists because we had total creative control and we delivered the laughs each night with no fear of repercussions from Comedy Central network executives."

"And that has obviously changed for Stephen now that he is hosting *The Late Show*?" asked Rose, a CBS employee at that time, addressing the transition.

"Of course," said Stewart.

"But now that Stephen has made the transition, and you are working on the show as well, is there a day that stands out for both of you? Is there an experience that you will both remember forever?"

Stewart just grinned and his smile grew wider thinking of one special evening which had become the favorite story for him and his pal Colbert.

"There is one story in particular that Stephen and I often bring up anytime we need a laugh," said Stewart, leaning back a bit in his chair, prepared to share this great story with the world for the first time. "This is back in November of 2012, late on a Friday evening when Stephen and I entered an Italian bistro after finishing the taping of our shows. We had just started a tradition of going out after the final show of the week."

On this Friday evening, the two tired national-comedy stars made their way to *Guido's Place*, a restaurant Stewart happened into about a month earlier after he had taken a wrong turn into a not so nice section of Hell's Kitchen off Eighth Avenue. That evening, the owner, one Guido Manilucci, offered him dinner on the house and asked for a photo he could hang up in the center of the restaurant's Wall of Fame with photos of the other celebrities that dined there.

This pleasant and affordable experience led Stewart to start frequenting the dining establishment, despite the neighborhood, decorum, food, and so on. Free food and his photo on the wall, why not? A few weeks later, he decided to make it *the* Friday dinner spot for him and his pal from South Carolina, and it quickly became their new tradition.

Guido, a lifelong New Yorker, spotted the two cable talk show giants entering the front door and quickly walked up to greet them.

"Hey Jon, Stephen, how's it going, eh?" said the middle-aged, overweight, mustached, and jovial owner with a heavy New York accent. "Ya know I got your favorite table open."

"Hey, thanks Guido," said Stewart, smiling, but looking tired from a tough week of being funny and smart, not easy in any business, but really difficult when a million people are watching you attempt it each night. "I am starved!"

"Me too!" said Colbert, following Stewart and Guido towards the back of the restaurant to a small table with two rickety old chairs in a corner with red brick walls on each side, decorated only by a few lit candles, some of which were duct taped to stay in place. "Why don't you have the chef start cookin' up our favorites?"

"Yes," added Stewart. "And I know Stephen and I would like a glass of your finest grape, as always, Guido my good man."

"Hey, dat sounds good Jon," said Guido, shrugging his shoulders, and then tilting his head from side to side, the nervous mannerisms he exhibited every time he addressed someone. "I will get on it right away. Youz twos guys go ahead and sit down. I'll have dat bottle of chardonnay out here before you can tuck your napkin in, you know? Hey, you know what I mean? Before you can tuck your napkin in. Know what I'm saying?"

"We got you, goombah," laughed Stewart, whose fairly large, nicely framed photo hung on the wall opposite his table. Guido was always eager to let guests know this was Jon Stewart's favorite hangout and THE table where he ate his meals. He never saw Jon's show, not once, but a former employee, a young bartender named Billy O'Donnell, filled him in the show and its famous host.

"Jon, when are they going to put my photo up there?" asked Colbert, looking at the Wall of Fame where Stewart's photo took the most prominent position at the center, surrounded by several other photos of local news celebrities in town. On the right of his signed Comedy Central mugshot was a framed Polaroid photo of Mike Smithson, an associate producer for the 5:00 a.m. news at WNBC-TV. To the left was a coffee-stained photo of Mary O'Neil, the receptionist at WOR-TV. And right below was a police lineup profile photo of the always recognized, Marty Forkin, who was the security guard at FOX News for about five weeks in the late 1990s. Yes, this was a group Stewart was proud to be among, no question about it.

Colbert struggled with the photo priority pecking order at the restaurant.

"I gave them a signed photo a few weeks ago," said *The Colbert Report's* star, not accustomed to being snubbed by anyone, especially the owner of a rat-infested restaurant.

"The photo is up Stephen," informed his pal. "I saw it. A beautiful spot, right over the urinal."

"Hah, hah, you are a funny man Jon," chuckled Colbert, organizing the salt and pepper shakers on the table so they were lined up perfectly with the napkin holder, showing early signs of possible OCD.

"I'm not kidding," he said with a straight face. "They have no idea who you are."

"What?"

"They had no idea who I was either until they hired a college kid to tend bar, who told them about me and the show. Unfortunately, Billy O'Donnell only lasted two days, because he couldn't converse with Guido and his staff about network TV shows like *COPS, Judge Judy,* and *Wheel of Fortune.* He never watched them. Too bad you weren't with me the first day I came here. Your picture would be right up there with mine for all of the half-wits, nitwits, and dimwits that come into this place to admire. Isn't that what it's all about?"

Colbert rolled his eyes, adjusted his glasses, and took a sip of the water, but he couldn't help but notice the waiter serving the food at a table in front of them. "Oh my God, it's him!"

Stewart looked over to see a dark-haired, overweight, forty-something waiter with a sagging and red-splotched apron around his waist serving the plates of pasta to an odd-looking couple a few tables away—an old businessman with a young woman that didn't seem to be his daughter.

"Do you think they know?" asked Stewart.

"No way," said Colbert, watching the waiter walk away from the couple's table, back toward the kitchen area. He stopped at a station that had stacked eight-ounce glasses and large plastic pitchers of water. "Here it comes."

"Wouldn't be any fun coming here if he didn't," said Stewart, who watched the waiter take a pitcher, pour a glass of water, then stand up straight, drinking the glass of water in his left hand, while he used his right hand to violently adjust his personal equipment, then readjust it.

Stewart and Colbert couldn't help laughing at this incredibly disgusting ritual which they had watched many times, but never had the heart to tell any of the other customers prior to being served.

"Oh, that's new!" said Colbert, seeing the waiter do a two-thumbed scratch of the lower groin, finishing with a satisfied and audible, "Ahhh!"

"He should write a book about best ways to scratch and adjust, don't you think Stephen?" asked Stewart. "I'd book 'em."

Guido returned to the table and showed the two political comedy news stars a bottle of chardonnay. "Hey, dis is some of our best stuff right here guys. Youz guys are gonna luv dis!"

Colbert looked at the label as Guido turned the twist cap off of the wine bottle, "Ah yes," he said. "2011 was a very good year! Last year, wasn't it?"

"I'm tellin' ya, you will luv dis!" said Guido. "Troot is, I don't 'xactly know where it comes from, but I know our guys get it off da back of a truck in da Bronx."

"May I sniff the twistoff cap?" asked Stewart, sharing his sarcastic humor with his comedy pal, knowing it would sail right over Guido's balding head. Colbert just put his head down and laughed, but stopped abruptly as a disturbing thought occurred to him.

"Hey Guido, I know you are aware of this, but just so there are no mixups," said the ultra-neat and clean Colbert with a look of concern on his face. "We always like you to serve our food, right? I mean, you know that, don't you?"

"I take great pride in serving youz two guys," said Guido, shifting his head from left to right again.

"We appreciate that," Stewart smiled. "We just wouldn't want that other waiter over there serving us, if it's okay with you?"

Guido looked back over his shoulder to see two waiters at the water station.

"Do you mean Bobby over there?" he asked, pointing correctly toward the culprit.

"Well, I don't know his name," said Stewart, seeing the waiter now demonstrating the two-hand grab and tug adjustment. "There, him! Tommy Tug-a-Lot over there."

"Yeah," Colbert laughed. "You know, the one now putting his hands down his pants."

Guido looked over at his waiter. "Hey Bobby," he yelled across the room. "Would you mind getting your damn hands outta your pants! This is a restaurant. People eat dat food ya serve."

The odd-looking couple that had just been served stopped mid-chew to look up at the waiter, saw him finishing an intense game of pocket pool, put their forks down, spit the food into their napkins, and called for the check.

"'Scuse me gents," said Guido, who went over to the table to talk to his now-sickened customers.

Colbert took a sip of the wine and remarked, "This is good, if you like turpentine."

"Oh, I love turpentine," quipped the graying *Daily Show* host, looking around to make sure no one could hear him, then spoke in a low tone of voice. "Hey Stephen, let me ask you a pretty sensitive question, if you don't mind?"

Colbert, realizing the funny had left the room for a moment and it was time for a serious conversation. "Sure, what's up?"

"Well, this must stay between you and me, right?"

Guido turned from the odd couple's table and said to Stewart, "Don't you mean to say, you and I? Ya know?"

"Wow, that's the worst case of elephant ears I've ever witnessed," said a concerned looking Stewart, who lowered his head and voice even further.

"Look, no problem Jon, go ahead," Colbert responded, confident he would keep any secret for the man who gave him one of his biggest breaks, when he hired him on *The Daily Show*.

"Well, we are both really funny, right?" Stewart began.

"We try," agreed Colbert.

"I mean, critics, viewers, everyone seems to think our shows are incredibly funny, right? That's the same input you get, isn't it? It's what we have heard for several years. It's why I get asked to host the Academy Awards and so on, right?"

"Yes, absolutely," Colbert agreed once more, now wondering where Jon was going with this line of questioning.

"Well, wouldn't you think one of the networks would have made one of us, or both of us, an offer by now to host one of the late night talk shows?" asked a bewildered-looking Stewart. "I mean let's be honest. I love Comedy Central and the opportunity they have given us, but it has somewhat of a limited reach, wouldn't you agree?"

Colbert sat and considered this logic for a moment, then said, "Jon, honestly, I think our shows are too irreverent, too controversial for the average network viewer. I don't think you can be as politically disruptive as we are when you are on one of the three major networks.

"You can't forget Jon, our humor and views appeal to a certain audience, college students, college graduates, liberal-minded people to be sure. A lot of the folks in the rural areas, and even the cities, don't get cable or satellite TV and depend on the networks for their programs. Do you really think a lot of those folks would like our humor? Heck no! They would hate us!"

Stewart knew his pal was right, but struggled with the idea that they weren't being offered those more prominent network slots; not to mention the big money!

Colbert continued, "The networks need someone who can appeal to that general audience. They need safer humor that will entertain without offending, while keeping the ratings."

"Even if they aren't that funny?" asked Stewart.

"Like who?" wondered Colbert, who certainly had his own list on the subject.

"Well, I don't want to name any names, but..." Stewart stopped when he saw two waiters including their favorite, Lance McItchy, walk past them carrying a very large golden frame toward the Wall of Fame. The two waiters placed the framed photo on the floor, leaning it against the wall, while they took down the four big local celebs, including Stewart, to make room. Then they hung the new photo.

"Hey excuse me, Max McScratcher, what are you doing?" asked Stewart, who was in no mood to see his photo removed from the wall of the Condessa Del Firetrap.

"Owner said we needs to put dis new one up," said the walking restaurant-code violation.

And there, taking Stewart's place on the wall, was an all-too-familiar face. It was a man that both he and Stephen called a friend, Conan O'Brien.

"Do you think they even know Conan?" asked Colbert.

"Not a chance," said Stewart.

❧

At this same moment in Beverly Hills, California, it was nearly 7:00 p.m. and Conan O'Brien had just finished taping his talk show, *Conan*, on TBS. For his final show of the week, he had interviewed Reese Witherspoon and then Portia de Rossi. The beautiful and always engaging Witherspoon had put O'Brien into a great mood which was quickly dissipated by de Rossi, who told an incredibly stupid story that went on and on about taking her dog for a walk, ending up at a friend's gated home, where she was not invited, but entered the grounds, where her dog got away, and a security camera followed her while she looked at the security pad on the stone fence column and, oh my goodness, O'Brien was ready to quit show the business listening to her.

Off to the sanctuary of the posh restaurant at the Beverly Hills Hotel where O'Brien was scheduled to meet his long-time friend, Robert Smigel, for dinner. The two successful comedy stars were greeted at the door immediately by a beautiful and sophisticated host named Barbara, who was surrounded by an always-professional staff, some of whom just happened to be big Conan O'Brien fans. One, a very cute blonde waitress, offered to show the famed talk show host and his friend to the best seat in the restaurant, looking out at the beautiful garden area which was lit wonderfully by the setting sun.

"Right this way Mr. O'Brien," said the waitress, dressed in a short, light-brown blazer, white-collared shirt, brown bow tie, and matching brown skirt, presenting a very impressive and professional-looking uniform.

"So honored to have you join us," said a beautiful brunette girl, who joined her associate to help seat O'Brien and his friend Smigel, whom they didn't recognize. The brunette waitress was a stunning beauty, who looked very much like international film star Angelina Jolie, and hoped she too would one day be starring in movies, not seating talk show hosts at a restaurant.

When they reached the soft, light-green, padded semi-circular booth, the blonde girl lost her composure for just a moment and made an inappropriate request, "Mr. O'Brien, would you mind?" she began, then looked like she was reconsidering her request. "Can you do the jump for me? Would you mind? I love the jump!"

The always-polite New Englander didn't blink, got into his low crouch with arms bent back for thrust and sprang forward, launching himself a full six inches, then spun pointing at the young lady. This was the routine that had become the Red-Haired Wonder's signature move, like legendary talk show host Johnny Carson's golf swing.

The celebrity frenzy had begun and the brunette was not to be denied. "Can I touch your…?" she asked holding her right hand out toward his famous red locks.

"Sure, why not?" he said, feeling her very lovely hand make its way through his thick, long, red hair. Somehow, this request was all-too familiar, and when beauties like this made the request, the great O'Brien had to remind himself about his lovely wife Liza and two young children, Neve and Beckett, back at home.

As he sat down, he began to wonder if Hollywood was becoming a prison for him. In New York, he could usually walk down the streets without too much harassment outside of, "Hi Conan! How's it going, Conan! Red Sox suck, Conan!" Although he was from Boston and a Red Sox fan, New Yorkers considered him one of them, which was a unique allowance for New Yorkers, especially when it comes to the Red Sox.

He often wondered if he should have gotten out of L.A. after being booted off *The Tonight Show* and launching *Conan* from Los Angeles back in November of 2010. O'Brien's friend, Smigel, had just flown in from New York to meet with him. Smigel was rarely recognized on the street. His success evolved from the legendary sketches he wrote for *Saturday Night Live* and later the off-beat *TV Funhouse* cartoon segments on *SNL* that had made his name famous. And if the young wait staff at the restaurant were to learn that Smigel was the creator of *Triumph the Insult Comic Dog*, all hell would break loose and he would be signing autographs for hours.

In an industry where true loyalty is rare, Conan felt a very strong bond to his dark, curly-haired, middle-aged friend, who was considered a genius by many in the entertainment industry. Smigel played a significant role in Conan's success, lobbying producer Loren Michaels during the summer of 1993 to hire his *SNL* writing buddy for the open *Late Night* host job, knowing Conan would excel in that chair. And when Conan was selected, Smigel joined him at *Late Night* to help make the show a success, with incredibly zany comedy bits that have become famous throughout America starting with the "lips" segments, which featured a large celebrity photo with the lips cut out, so Smigel could mouth crazy dialogue in a conversation with Conan.

Many at *SNL* believed that Conan was born to be a talk show host, recognizing O'Brien's ability to talk to people, interview them, sincerely listening and staying within the moment of the conversation, following up with good questions pertaining directly to the specific details being shared during that moment. His talent wasn't necessarily that of a great standup comedian. It was his people skills and interview skills, plus knowing how to play his part within a comedy bit, that made him special.

O'Brien could never touch the talents of seasoned standup comedians like Jay Leno or David Letterman, or the great comic talents of Stephen Colbert or Jon Stewart for that matter. No, the Red-Haired Wonder's talents become apparent the second he sits in the talk show host's chair, where his genuinely warm personality and likeability shine through.

So there he sat in the Beverly Hills Hotel restaurant, looking over the menu, when a waiter, who had just moved to L.A. from New York, approached them.

"Hello Mr. O'Brien and Mr. Smigel! I am Billy O'Donnell and I will be helping to serve you today," said the smiling young Harvard grad, who had aspirations of writing television shows or movies.

"Thanks, Billy," said Conan, also a Harvard man, who graduated magna cum laude and was the editor of the *Harvard Lampoon*. "Well, I know Robert and I would like to try a bottle of your best California Chardonnay, and some calamari would be terrific as well."

"Very good sir, I will be right back with your drinks and appetizer," he said, then quickly walked to the kitchen. As he entered the right side of the set of swinging kitchen doors, out stepped the cute blonde girl from the left side, carrying a basket of fresh rolls.

"Here you go gentlemen," she said, the smell of the wonderful oven-baked bread filling the air around them. "And as I mentioned, I am a huge fan of yours and hope you don't mind if I pass along my resume and audition DVD." Out of a large pocket in her apron, blondie pulled out a DVD in a colorful plastic case with her name across the front, Whisper Stream.

"Oh, thank you," said Conan, looking at the cover and laughing a bit. "I don't suppose that's really your name, is it?"

"Yes, yes it is," she said, lifting her chin proudly, trying to hide the hurt she was feeling from the question. "My parents knew I would one day become a major movie star, so they gave me that name so I wouldn't have to think of a stage name later."

"Good thinking," said Smigel, trying not to laugh and further offend her.

"Thank you for looking at it," she said. "I can't let them see me talking to you like this. I'll get in trouble." She left and quickly disappeared through the kitchen door, just as the brunette girl came out the other side and walked directly to Conan's table.

"Here is the butter and your butter knives," she said with a wonderful look that had such a tremendous star-quality to it. Smigel and Conan nodded as she walked away, but she quickly turned and came back to the table.

"I apologize," she said with a very serious look on her face. "That was not the proper way for me to present you with the butter." She picked up the butter tray, lifted it up near her face and started singing to the music of the song "I'm So Pretty" from West Side Story as she danced around the table.

"Here's the butter, tasty butter,
Here's the butter, the butter today!
Here's your butter, and it's going to be a tasty day.
La, la, la, la, la, la la, la, la, la!"

"Veronica!" a loud voice blasted across the room from the hostess Barbara.

The singer froze, "Sorry!" Then she addressed the two men. "Gotta go," and off she scampered.

O'Brien sat there with a puzzled look on his face. First, he had to endure Portia de Rossi's boring story on the show that night, then have an audition DVD shoved at him by a woman with a strange name whom he just offended, followed by an unscheduled performance from an Angelina Jolie look-alike doing her rendition of "Butter" from West Side Story.

"Robert, did this ever happen to us in New York?" asked the tall, pale-faced talk show host, who looks like he should be the spokesperson for the country of Ireland, providing America with its greatest product—talented and hard-working people.

"Not that I can remember," said his long-time Jewish friend, who had grown up in Manhattan, but moved to Chicago to train in improvisational comedy, and introduced a long-running sketch-comedy show titled, *All You Can Eat and The Temple of Doom.*

The two men knew these intrusions would not continue and the dining experience would most definitely get better at this exclusive establishment. It did.

Waiter Billy O'Donnell returned in a very professional manner, showed the two gentlemen the bottle of Robert Mondavi Private Label Chardonnay, operating the cork screw like a pro, quickly opening the bottle and presenting the cork to Conan to sniff, while pouring a small sample into Mr. Smigel's glass for him to taste. The gentlemen nodded their approval, and young O'Donnell poured them both a half glass of wine, placing the bottle into the metal bucket of ice to keep it properly chilled. "Very good gentlemen," he said in a professional tone, then pulled a fairly thick script out of his jacket and handed it to Conan saying, "And if you have a few minutes, perhaps you can take a read of my script, which would make a wonderful television movie."

All of a sudden, O'Brien felt a little numb as he looked up at this nice young fellow, while hoping all the while he would have a chance to have dinner with his friend and discuss his continuing thoughts about moving back to New York.

"Uh, yeah Billy, I'll take a read, when I get a chance, thanks," said an always polite O'Brien, just as his mother had taught him growing up in the suburbs of Boston.

"Thanks," said O'Donnell, who turned very professionally and walked back toward the kitchen.

⁂

Back at *Guido's Place* in New York, Stewart and Colbert were continuing their lament about their lack of big time network offers when they were approached once again by the jovial Italian owner.

"Here ya go gents," he said, placing the hot, steaming food on the table in front of them. "Pasta Fazul for you Jon and a plate of Lasagna for you Mr. Colbert." After he placed the plates down he saw the two waiters at the Wall of Fame stacking up the photos they took down.

"Nice photo of Conan, don't ya tink fellas?" Guido asked his two irritated customers.

"Yeah, great," said Colbert. "Does he eat here?"

"No, but I was told by a guy dat if we put his photo up, people will tink he does. Good for business, ya know."

"Yeah, great!" Colbert agreed. "Conan's a pretty funny guy, huh?"

"Conan?"

"Yeah," said Colbert, trying to find out if the owner even knew him.

"Never watch 'em," admitted Guido. "Personally, I run widda certain crowd, ya know? We love DeNiro in *Analyze Dis* and *Analyze Dat*! Now dat's funny stuff!"

"Those are funny movies," said Stewart. "But no one here has ever watched *Conan* on TBS or when he was hosting *The Tonight Show* or *Late Night*?"

"Is that the red-haired guy?" asked Guido, looking at the picture. "Oh wait, I have watched him. I guess I didn't put it together. Yeah, I love when he does that jump," he said, then tried to re-enact Conan's signature move.

"Wow that was pretty…uh…pretty something," Colbert said, amazed at how silly the owner looked trying to recreate the famous move.

"Yeah, I like dat guy," said Guido. "He's funny!"

Then something occurred to Colbert, "Guido, do you get cable here?"

"We used to," said the smiling Italian native. "But the cable company found out and tried to charge us for it. Can you believe dat? I told 'em, I got your sixty-eight fifty right here!" he said grabbing his cable package and shaking it.

"Hey Guido, where da ya want deez?" asked Fingers McLugnuts, carrying the photos he had taken down from the wall.

"Urinal!" said Guido without skipping a beat.

Stewart and Colbert gave each other a look of great surprise.

"Urinal, nice!" said Colbert. "We'll be together again Jon. Just you and me, side by side above the urinals."

"Hey, I want the first urinal," said Stewart, his sarcasm once again escaping the owner. "If I can't have the first pisser, I want no pisser at all."

"Isn't that what Nathan Hale once said?" quipped Colbert.

"No, I think that was Nathan Lane," the diminutive comedy host joked back. "Well Guido, we can't thank you enough for the wonderful meals you have provided to us free of charge over the last month, but I have to say, this will be our last."

"Whad da ya kiddin?" he chuckled, thinking this was a joke.

"No, I can live with disgusting waiters and stolen wine, but I draw the line at having my photo hung over a urinal," explained Stewart with a smile, but actually quite serious this time.

"Hey I'm sorry Jon, I didn't tink you'd mind," said Guido. "I mean most of the guys dat come in here will see ya in dere, ya know?"

"I know, it's a great spot," said Stewart. "But I think Stephen and me…"

"Stephen and I, ya mean," interrupted Guido, raising his right index finger to correct the mistake.

"Right, forgot I was talking with an English major. Stephen and I will try some new restaurant next time. Yes, something new and different, maybe a restaurant without code violations, rat-infested walls, good food, real wine, that kind of thing."

"Right," said Guido, not too happy to receive so many sarcastic shots aimed at his restaurant.

"But thank you for this truly memorable experience," said Stewart, looking over at Colbert who had a concerned look on his face.

"Sure, why not? You go do dat," he said now visibly angry, watching the two gentlemen stand up to leave. "And you go ahead and forgetta about us too, okay? Capeesh?"

"Capeesh," said Stewart, now realizing he had gone too far and offended Guido, which was not a great idea in that part of town. He reached out to shake the owner's hand, "Hey, no hard feelings, eh Guido?"

Guido just looked at Stewart's hand, then over at his two waiters, who knew what that look meant and started toward Comedy Central's two greatest investments.

"Yeah, we got to go," said Colbert and the two men quickly, very quickly, walked, then ran out the door, knowing they had better be more careful about taking shots at Italian restaurant owners in Hell's Kitchen.

As they walked down a darkened Eighth Avenue, a shaken Stewart turned to his pal, "Stephen, I think we should just move our shows to the West coast, don't you?" he said still breathing hard from the narrow escape. "Fresh air. Beautiful women everywhere. No one bothering us. Wouldn't that be the life?"

❧

Whisper Stream placed the dinner plates in front of O'Brien and Smigel and said, "Please gentlemen, let me know if there is anything else I can get you." She smiled and slowly backed up a few steps, seemingly not to disturb them any further. As Conan began cutting into his very tender, medium-rare, eight-ounce filet mignon, Whisper Stream, asked, "How is your steak, Mr. O'Brien?" But her voice was different. It was sort of a monotone and had a rhythm to it.

"Oh, it looks good," he said indicating she had asked the question just a bit too early.

"I had a steak earlier today too! Actually, I had two steaks. Had two steaks today," she said in that same monotone voice in that same rhythm. Smigel and O'Brien immediately recognized what was happening. Good ol' Whisper Stream was doing an audition piece for them of "Penelope the One-Upper," the character made famous by Kristen Wiig on *Saturday Night Live.*

Smigel tried to help his friend, "Look Whisper, Conan's had a long day and if it's okay with you, we would just like to have our dinner in peace and quiet. You know, no interruptions."

"I had no interruptions today," she continued, profusely annoying them with the character imitation. "None at all, far fewer than you."

From the kitchen emerged the young Irish writer O'Donnell, who looked like he would provide some assistance. "Whisper," he said, sounding stern and determined. "I hope you are conducting yourself appropriately here."

The actress just looked at him and started to speak, when he cut her off, asking, "Have you asked Mr. O'Brien if you could read the first few pages of my script to him? Have you? Hmmm? I think these two gentlemen would enjoy it."

Smigel looked back for the hostess, hoping to put an end to this unscheduled audition and script-reading. When he turned to look, he saw Veronica the singing waitress and four very effervescent smiling waiters, wearing top hats and carrying black canes, walking right behind her. Before Smigel could raise his hand to signal for help, Veronica broke into song he had never heard before, obviously an original tune.

"I'm here for you,
To sing and dance.
And I'm going to make you smile,
While I sing and dance!"

As she belted out her tune, the smiling dancers accompanying her, held the brim of their top hats with their left hand, as they mirrored the choreographed dance kicks of their star singer in her first performance at the Beverly Hills Hotel.

"I was in a song and dance number once," said Whisper, while Veronica and her backup dancers continued the big production number. "Actually, I was on Broadway in the *Chorus Line*, which is better. Ran four years."

After the first verse, Veronica joined the line in the middle of her four dancers. Then, Billy O'Donnell moved quickly to join the line on one end, while Whisper jumped in at the other end, saying, "I can sing too! I'm a great singer, wonderful singer."

Veronica cut right to the big finish, all seven of them kicking their legs like The Rockettes at Radio City Music Hall as Veronica belted out,

"Oh my! I really have to mention,
Please don't have, any apprehension,
To book me today!"

The Red-Haired Wonder watched this Hollywood lunacy for a moment, then at his untouched delicious-looking steak. He picked up his napkin and threw it on his plate.

"Robert, I think I have to move back east to New York," said Conan, standing and walking toward the exit with his friend right beside him, nodding in agreement. "Real people! Energy of the city! Beautiful women everywhere! No one bothering me. Wouldn't that be the life?"

❧

Charlie Rose placed his right hand on his face, laughing his silent laugh, having enjoyed Stewart's story. "That is an incredible tale," said Rose.

"Yes, and as you know, Conan ultimately decided not to move back East, preferring to keep his kids in the same area, same schools, not disrupt their lives. He and his wife are great parents."

"And David Letterman decided to called it quits and Stephen did get the job," said Rose.

"Yes, which we were obviously thrilled about," said Stewart about his loyal pal. "He's really having a blast doing the bits on Trump."

Rose laughed and concluded the interview.

"Well, thank you Jon for sharing that incredible story. Really fascinating!" said Rose, turning to look directly toward the camera. "Next week, our guests will be Harvey Weinstein and Louis C.K., who will tell us about a new organization they have founded to help men like themselves. It's called Perverts Anonymous. I'll personally be very interested in hearing about it. See you then."

CHAPTER 15

THE NAKED TRUTH ABOUT MATT LAUER

Did NBC executives know about longtime *Today Show* host Matt Lauer's history of sexual harassment at the network prior to the story being broken on November 29, 2017? Certainly, NBC executives had plenty of clues, plenty of information years ago about Lauer's inappropriate behavior. Some point to interviews Lauer conducted with Sandra Bullock about her naked scene in the 2009 movie, *The Proposal.* One inside source said that NBC executives must have known from a story Lauer planned during the November of 2008 Sweeps Weeks ratings battle, when it seemed very apparent to several *Today* staffers.

The battle that takes place between television network morning shows has always been highly competitive with executives at each network trying to develop unique, sexy, or controversial stories that will draw viewers and win the ratings war. There have been many incredible stories that have come out of these ratings wars, but none quite like what happened during the November 2008 Sweeps Weeks in which Lauer played a leading role.

Back then, *The Today Show* absolutely dominated the ratings, drawing more than five and a half million viewers each morning. *Good Morning America* closed the gap every now and then, but always seemed to be lagging about a million and a half viewers behind, while *CBS This Morning*, always last, pulled about two and a half million.

The *GMA* producers believed that their morning show was just as good as *The Today Show*, but regardless of how hard they worked, they were never able to pull that steadfast group of loyal viewers away from *Today's* co-hosts Matt Lauer, Meredith Vieira, Ann Curry, and Al Roker.

Gina Tully was a senior at New York's Columbia University studying journalism with the hope of one day becoming an on-air reporter. An internship was the final requirement for her degree and she was lucky enough to receive an unpaid internship at *The Today Show* beginning on August 15, 2008, and scheduled to finish December 10, when she would receive her diploma in the graduation commencement ceremony at Columbia's Westside campus.

Like so many interns, Gina's job at *Today* covered the gamut of answering phones, making copies, getting coffee, doing some shopping for some of the on-air staff; anything that was asked of her. She watched the segment producers and executive producers each day, hoping someday that she would be in their shoes, producing stories that the entire nation would watch. But her aspirations grew even greater during her time at the network. She grew to admire Meredith Vieira and Ann Curry and hoped one day to become a co-host on a morning show, just like them.

At approximately 11:30 a.m. on Monday during the final week of October, the Columbia student answered the phone in what turned out to be a very strange conversation, one she would have normally hung up on fairly quickly. However, this man got her attention.

"*Today Show*," said Gina with as much politeness as possible, given the fact that it seemed like the 300th time she had stated the show's name while answering calls that morning.

"Hello, may I speak with Gina Tully?" the man asked, peaking Gina's curiosity since she didn't recognize the voice at all.

"This is Gina, who is calling?" she asked.

"Oh, hello Gina," said a deep gruff male voice. "This is David Finney from the Citizens for Better Television, how are you today?"

"Fine thank you, what can I do for you Mr. Finney?" she said, realizing this was a call that she would have to be careful handling, since it sounded like it was coming from a television watchdog advocacy group.

"Ms. Tully, we know that you have been working at *Today* as an intern for over two months now and I would like to meet with you to discuss an opportunity," said Finney, with the sound of honking cars in the background which indicated that he was probably calling from a cellphone somewhere in Manhattan.

"A job opportunity?" she asked, now really curious about where this call was leading and how he knew about her tenure at the show.

"I would call it more of a project, but it is quite a good opportunity," he explained. "Would you be available to meet me at the Starbucks at Fifty-Second and Eighth Avenue, right around the corner from *The Ed Sullivan Theater*, tomorrow morning at eleven o'clock?"

Gina, dressed in long heavy black overcoat, gloves, and French beret, entered the Starbucks that very cold Tuesday morning. She looked around for someone to identify themselves. She was tired, having worked since 5:00 a.m., but she spotted a man seated at one of the tall round tables toward the back of the coffee shop, raising his right hand and waving her over to him. Gina walked toward him, taking off her gloves, trying to absorb as much as possible about this salt-and pepper-bearded, middle-aged man wearing a black fedora, tan overcoat, and sunglasses. Sunglasses? This was strange given the gray overcast day. As she approached the table, he stood and reached out to shake her hand.

"Hello Gina, I'm David Finney," he said. "Thank you for meeting with me today."

"Thanks, Mr. Finney," she replied politely, sitting down at the table. "I found your organization's website, but the information was rather vague about what exactly you do."

"Yes, thank you Gina," said Finney, returning to his wooden chair. "Well, to put it simply, our purpose is to help influence networks to produce quality television, shows that are educational as well as entertaining."

"That sounds good," she said. "So why did you want to see me?"

"Well, we have several clients who share the same mission as our group," he said.

"Clients?" she asked. "Why would an advocacy group have clients? Don't you just have supporters?

"Supporters, clients, sponsors, they're all pretty much the same thing," he explained. "We all want quality television and, whereas our job is to go out and implement the communications programs to bring that about, the clients provide the means to produce those programs. Without them, we wouldn't be able to do our jobs."

"Propaganda programs? Is that what you're talking about?" she asked, now a bit skeptical about Mr. Finney and his true intentions for the meeting.

"We currently have a very important project, which we believe you could help us implement," he said, taking out a yellow notepad and pen. "I assume you are currently working to prepare for Sweeps Weeks at *Today*."

"Every day, night and day," she said. "I guess I never realized the amount of work news shows put in to prepare for these ratings weeks. It's incredible!"

"Yes, and as the leader in the morning news ratings," Finney continued. "You know how important it is to produce a quality product that will maintain that leadership."

"That's what I am learning," she said.

"Well, my client is working hard to attain the same standards as *Today*, the same quality of segments," he said, but was cut off again by a somewhat agitated Tully.

"Your client again!" she said. "Who is your client?"

"Well, let's just say they are in the same business as *Today* and would very much like to deliver high quality television news on par, or even better than, what *Today* is planning on producing during this upcoming ratings period."

Gina stood up. "Are you with *Good Morning America*?" she asked, now feeling panicked as though she had just crossed the line of some great journalistic trust. "*CBS This Morning*, are they your client?"

"Please Gina, allow me to finish," he implored of her. "I think once you have heard what I have to say, you will be very happy you took this meeting."

Gina slowly sat back down, hoping there was some good reason she didn't run out the door and back to her safe newsroom desk in Rockefeller Center.

"My client is *Good Morning America*, which is a high-quality television news program, as you well know," he continued. "*GMA* would like to win this ratings period outright, beating *Today*, where you have worked for the past couple months as an unpaid intern."

"How do you know that?" she asked.

"You are scheduled to finish the second week of December, just after the ratings period," he continued.

"How do you know this?" she demanded, standing this time determined to leave, as she grabbed her gloves off the table. People around them began to notice the disturbance and watched in concern.

"Please sit," he pleaded once again, grabbing her arm in a non-threatening fashion, hoping she would stay. She stood there looking at this strange man for a moment, then somewhat reluctantly sat back down. A young, Irish-looking gentleman in a blue business suit sitting a few tables away, placed his hands on the round table, ready to step in and intercede if the bearded middle-aged man touched the young lady again.

"It's my business to know these things," he continued cautiously, looking over at the twenty-something Irish businessman. "Once your internship ends in December, you are free to work for any other network.

"Except, I am expecting *Today* to hire me after graduation," she vigorously interrupted.

"They are going to hire you?" he asked sounding quite skeptical.

"Absolutely, I will have put in almost four months of unpaid work by then," said Gina confidently, turning to smile at the Irishman letting him know everything was fine. "They all like me there very much, especially Meredith Vieira, and since she is one of the stars of the show as a co-host, that has to help."

"Have they talked to you about a paid position yet?" he asked.

"No, they haven't, but I think they are waiting until the final week," she said, knowing the odds were against her getting a full-time position at *Today*, but did believe she would be offered a part-time position as a segment producer.

"You have a much better chance of getting hired at *Good Morning America* than you do at *Today* and that is all part of the opportunity I am here to talk to you about this morning," he explained, now getting her full attention.

"Really?" she asked.

Finney leaned in and spoke at a much lower level so only Gina could hear, "We believe at Citizens for Better Television that if our client at *GMA* were to attain *Today's* production plan and schedule, it would help them meet their objective. Is that something you could provide to me at Citizens for Better Television?"

Gina leaned in and spoke in a whisper, "Are you asking me if I can I get my hands on the segments planned and the days and times those segments will run?"

"Exactly," he said, pointing his index finger toward her, indicating that she had just hit the nail on the head.

"Yes, I could easily get that information," she whispered, looking around to see if anyone was listening. "But just to be clear. This isn't about *GMA* trying to create a higher quality of television. Aren't you just asking me to get this information, so they can run similar segments as *Today*?"

"Yes, that's exactly what we would like you to do," he said, confident she now had a full understanding of his objective for the meeting. Mr. Finney looked over to the Irishman who had returned to reading his *Wall Street Journal*.

"Well isn't that just a bit unethical, not to mention illegal?" she whispered, trying not to be heard by those around them.

Finney leaned in farther, his face only a foot away from the young intern, "Does *Today* have their interns sign any type of confidentiality agreement, whereby you can't share information about the show with anyone outside of the network?"

"If they do, they didn't make me sign it," she whispered even softer, knowing where he was going with this question.

"Exactly," he said, now smiling. "Which means you are free to pass along any information about the show to whomever you please; freedom of speech. I love that amendment!"

"Wow!" she said realizing he was right.

Within minutes, Gina was negotiating a deal with Mr. Finney that would give her a nice start in the television news business at ABC. She got the mysterious-looking bearded man to agree to a 75,000 dollar fee plus a full-time segment producer position at *GMA* with at least two on-air reporting opportunities each month for ABC's *World News Tonight*, the top of the mountain for any television news reporter. Mr. Finney said he would have to clear it with his client and would meet her again the next day.

Gina returned to the Starbucks the next morning and soon found herself at the same table with Mr. Finney, who handed her a thick yellow envelope filled with cash, equaling half the amount agreed to. She would receive the second payment and employment contract when she provided *Today's* Sweeps Weeks' programming information.

Walking back to her desk in the network's newsroom, she wondered if she was making a terrible mistake, crossing such a serious ethical line. Before going any further, she thought she had better give *Today* the benefit of the doubt. She approached the desk of executive producer, Ken Bowers, who looked quite busy at his computer, typing furiously.

"Have you got a minute, Mr. Bowers?" she asked politely, realizing she was interrupting Bowers, an out-of-shape veteran newsman, whose white dress shirt seemed to always be hanging out of his oversized, worn out black slacks.

"Not really, Gina," he said, glancing up at her, and quickly combing his oily black hair back from his forehead with is right hand. "I've got to finish this memo. It's really important. Sorry!"

"Okay, well quick question for you," she said, not letting that stop her. "Who should I talk to about a full-time position once I am done with my internship here?"

Now completely irritated with her obnoxious intrusion, Bowers stopped typing and looked up at her, "Full-time position? Are you kidding? You're an intern, right?"

"Yes, an unpaid intern for the past few months, staying late, coming in early, whatever was asked of me," she said, detailing the specific effort she had made for the show.

"Well, I hate to burst your bubble, Gina, but most interns don't get offered full-time positions here," he said, with an incredibly annoyed tone in his voice, as if she were infringing on the Holy Grail of news organizations. "You should view this as an honor to work here at *Today*, a privilege, a great addition to your resume. If they were going to offer you a job, I promise you, they would have talked to you by now. So if you don't mind, I have to get this done. Thank you."

Gina felt a numbness fill her entire body as she stood in front of the executive producer, feeling as though she had been used by the network. She had put in long hours, extra hours, trying to do a good job, show them that she would go the extra mile to get the job done. But obviously, no one at *Today* cared.

Somehow, she just couldn't accept it. She had gotten to know the popular morning co-host Meredith Vieira pretty well in her time at the show and liked her very much. She had personally gone out and shopped for Vieira and received great praise for her choices and efficiency. Certainly Meredith would provide a more positive picture. It was only a few minutes later that Gina was presenting her appeal to the highly Q-rated news celebrity.

"Gina, you know I like you very much and you have done a wonderful job here at *The Today Show*," said Meredith, with a very sympathetic tone in her voice, the same look and tone viewers had become accustomed to seeing each day. "Unfortunately, I don't have any say about who gets hired."

Now Gina was really devastated. First, she was rejected by the executive producer for whom she had worked long hours and done anything he asked of her. And now, the great Meredith Vieira was unable to help her.

Gina's disappointment only motivated her to get her hands on the Sweeps Weeks' production schedule as quickly as possible. She marched back to her tiny cubicle, sat at her computer and knew right where to find the information that would put a smile on the faces of those at *Good Morning America*. The schedule was only accessible by a few top-level producers on the show, but one of those producers made the mistake of asking Gina to call it up on her computer one day for him, which provided her with all the information she needed to pull up the Excel document anytime she wished. And on this day, she wished to pull it up plenty.

She quickly looked at the entire document which listed the production schedule for the Sweeps Weeks' segments to be produced, the reporter assigned to each story, and the day and time each story would be run. Gina placed a thumb drive into her computer and within seconds saved the entire file.

The next day, she was back at Starbucks with Mr. Finney, who ordered a grande vanilla latte while she filled out the paperwork required for new employees at ABC. She handed him the thumb drive, which he quickly checked on his laptop, then handed her the final yellow envelope, which she peeked into, making sure the money was there. It was that simple. This transaction could determine which network would win the ratings war and, in turn, millions of advertising dollars.

When Gina returned to the station, she entered the building with a huge chip on her shoulder, eager to help take *The Today Show* down in the ratings battle. She had already provided the programming schedule to *GMA*, but she went into the planning log to see if there was any other damage she could do. She knew how important the first segment would be for the media, saw the location of the segment, did some quick research and changed the shoot location from Miami to St. Petersburg, where a very interesting convention was taking place.

On Monday, November 3, the first day of Sweeps and one day before the historical Presidential election, the highly powerful and influential reporters who cover the media sat in their respective offices, each with four television sets in front of them to watch what the popular morning news programs would produce in order to win the big money at stake in the ratings battle. These reporters knew all too well that the main competition was between *Today* and *GMA*.

Meredith Vieira led off *The Today Show* reading all of the important breaking news, ending it with the most important story to which they would devote an entire segment.

"Tomorrow is election day and the two candidates, John McCain and Barack Obama are running very close in the polls," Vieira began with great energy, supported by the network's familiar symphony drum music in the background.

"President Bush announced a major change in his administration by withdrawing five thousand troops from Iraq, reducing U.S. presence even further in that country. But our top story today, how to make great tapioca pudding. And, does tapioca pudding lead to a better sex life?"

Yes, the Sweeps Weeks were off and running. While Vieira led into the all-important tapioca pudding sex segment, *GMA*'s co-host Diane Sawyer was able to land an exclusive interview with Senator Obama to ask what he thought his chances were to win the Presidency. Despite some of the polls and negative commentary, which predicted him losing, he was quite optimistic and believed he would win. It was a great interview and clearly a victory for *GMA*, as the media reporters kept score: *GMA* 1, *Today* 0.

Immediately after Sawyer finished her report, they did not break for a commercial like *Today* and *CBS This Morning*. Instead, Sawyer turned away from the screen where Senator Obama had just appeared, looking directly into camera one and saying, "And now we have a special segment we think you will all enjoy," she said with a big smile. "Our dare-devil co-host, Chris Cuomo, is coming to us live from the deck of a speed boat off the coast of Miami where he will attempt a parasailing adventure to see just how dangerous it really is for us regular folks. Is this something we should consider?"

The *GMA* director then cut to the live feed of Cuomo strapped into a harness about to be pulled up by a powerful sixty-foot bright yellow speed boat. "Thanks, Diane," said the young, fit, good-looking, shirtless, dark-haired newsman, dressed only in a blue Nike bathing suit and a big smile as he stood on the back of the boat. "I have always wanted to try this and today I get to find out just how brave I am, right?"

The boat began moving with a cameraman on deck and two small cameras placed on the ropes in front of Cuomo.

One of the cameras was pointed at him with the other directed downward to get a shot of the shore, showing viewers what he was looking at while in the air. Another camera was positioned on a boat a few hundred yards away, which showed the smiling and muscular ABC reporter rising off the deck and quickly up into the air. When he was several hundred feet in the air, he addressed his audience, "We chose Miami Beach because of the beautiful beaches and coastline."

The camera showed Miami Beach where about fifty sunbathers, all of them young women, were lying on beach chairs or wading into the cool shallow water. And every one of them looked like a supermodel! The young women were so beautiful and physically blessed; it looked like a beauty convention had been organized.

"Yes, this is the land of the beautiful people and I think I may have one of the best vantage points up here," said Cuomo, as he stared down toward the beach of bikini beauties, spotting a large sign planted in the sand that read, 'Hooters Mania.' "Yes Diane, I think I may have lucked into a Hooters Convention at 7:10 in the morning! What are the chances? I think our camera up here is able to show this to our viewers, who I believe will agree, it's quite a sight!"

Every second of the feed was carried live from Cuomo's harness cam. The *GMA* producers were tipped off by a friendly intern about the Hooters Convention only a few days earlier, which was paying big dividends for ABC.

Today came back from their commercial break and Meredith Vieira introduced the next segment. "It is quarter past the hour here at *The Today Show* and as you know we like to send my co-host, Matt Lauer, everywhere to see the world and try new things out," she said with a giddy smile, as she saw a producer out of the corner of her eye, trying to mouth something to her. "Today, we have sent Matt to the sunny coast of St. Pete, Florida where he is going to try parasailing. Here is our brave boy live from the deck of a speedboat. I understand this segment was your idea Matt."

"Yes Meredith, I felt the sights we could show from a few hundred feet in the air would be very interesting to our viewers," said Lauer, thinking he would soon be sailing over a group of Hooters models, a segment he had personally requested. "I've always wanted to try parasailing, so I'm very excited right now to get started."

The director went to a live shot of the balding, middle-aged, but still fit, Matt Lauer in a tank top and tight black Speedo swimming trunks, sitting in a harness on the deck of an old, but fairly fast, forty-foot orange speed boat operated by a seventy-year-old captain. "Well, I have done a lot of crazy things for this show, but I have to tell you, I am more frightened of parasailing today than the day I went skydiving with a man strapped to my back."

"Bet you loved that, eh Matt," said his weatherman pal, Al Roker, unable to let that line go by without taking a quick shot at his buddy.

"Oh thanks Al," smiled Matt. "I'd laugh but I'm too busy here in the warm sun, overlooking the beautiful blue ocean, while you are stuck in the freezing temperatures."

Meredith Vieira interjected, "Well, we can strap a man on your back again if you're more comfortable Matt?" she laughed. "By the way, weren't you able to find a pair of swimming trunks that fit a little better, more appropriately. After all, this is a family show."

"Yes, and that's why I just wanted to be sure if I landed in the water, they wouldn't come flying off me," said Lauer, laughing with a somewhat sinister smile.

"By the looks of them, I'm sure they won't," Vieira said sarcastically.

"Yes, now if we can get back to the story," continued Lauer. "Our viewers should know that this is a powerful speedboat that will send me eight hundred feet high over the pristine beaches of St. Petersburg, Florida, where I believe we will have a birds-eye view of some spectacularly beautiful sights on the beach."

Back in the studio, the producer with the concerned look on her face, ran over to the executive producer, Ken Bowers, to let him know *GMA* had just run the same exact segment. Too late! They had to go with it.

The boat sped up and the network news veteran was lifted off the deck easily and soared quickly into the blue skies over St. Pete. Like Cuomo, Matt Lauer had a cameraman positioned on the speed boat, one on a boat a few hundred yards away, and two mini-cams mounted to his harness. The view showed the white sandy beaches of St. Pete, which also had sunbathers scattered across it at 7:15 a.m., unusual to be sure. As Lauer looked down however, he didn't see the Hooters girls he had expected to be there. No, there was a large group of retirees sunbathing on the beach.

"Oh my God!" said a surprised Matt Lauer, realizing what he was viewing on the beach, then saw a large sign planted in the sand saying *Snowbirds Mania*. Lauer, forgetting for a moment that his microphone was on said, "Oh that's not right. Where's the Hooters girls?"

"What is it, Matt?" asked Meredith, watching the shot of Lauer's face turning white.

"Well, I hate to report this, Meredith, but I think there's been a mistake," said a highly disappointed Matt Lauer. "I'm looking down on a large group of senior citizens sunbathing where there was supposed to be a Hooters Convention."

"Hooters Convention?" asked Vieira.

"Yes, at least that what I thought would be down there. I mean, I was told..."

The director cut to the shot of five old, bald, pregnant-looking men standing together on the beach, conversing about something while smoking their cigars. One of the men toward the middle of the group started scratching himself like he had the worst case of fleas south of the border.

"There you go, Meredith," laughed Matt. "There's your Prince Charming waiting for you. And while he's waiting, he figures he'll scratch the fleas and ticks off himself."

A look of disbelief crossed Vieira's face.

"Seriously," continued Lauer. "I hate to report this, but I think we are passing over a convention of retirees. Can we give the producer that placed us in the wrong location an Emmy? Or perhaps a kick in the pants and a pink slip?"

The director pulled away from that shot and went to a group of old, wrinkled, overly-tanned women in bikinis, wearing large brimmed straw hats, extra-large sunglasses, and two-inch high heels as they laid on their beach chairs, sipping coffee.

"Why?" said Meredith, looking toward the director in the booth. "Why would you do that? And what's with the high heels?"

The segment finally came to an end with a very pale-looking Matt Lauer descending onto the speedboat, while the collective sound of channel controllers across the country were switching to *Good Morning America*, as the media critics adjusted their scorecards to read, *GMA* 15, *Today* –2 with notes wondering how they came up with the same type of story. Were they copying *GMA*?

As *Today* went to a commercial and screaming producers and co-hosts begged to find out who planned that segment, a young smiling intern sat in her cubicle watching and laughing to herself. But she knew the show was just getting started. Ah, revenge was sweet!

Executive producer Bowers was upset, but not defeated. He knew he had a segment in the can that would send their ratings over the top. They had an exclusive interview with movie star Angelina Jolie in her home, showing that she can cook. This blockbuster segment was taped in Hollywood only a week earlier and would come right after the news break at 8:00 p.m.

Just as *The Today Show's* beautiful brunette news anchor, Ann Curry, read the news, the face of Diane Sawyer came up on *Good Morning America* with a startling announcement, "This will be a great surprise to all of our viewers, but here today, live in our studio, we have with us Brad Pit and Angelina Jolie to finally clear up once and for all, why Brad left Jennifer Aniston for Angelina."

"I loved Jennifer," said Brad, fighting back the tears. "I still love her. Angelina knows that. Everyone thinks the breakup was due to Jennifer not wanting to have kids. And that was compounded by me and Angelina going out and adopting a large number of children to start our family.

"But the truth is that Jennifer can't cook. She can't cook at all. Sure, she was able to make me my favorite banana milkshake. That was easy! But when it came to cooking spaghetti and meatballs, no way. She just couldn't do it."

Diane Sawyer looked miffed as she asked, "But it's well known throughout Hollywood, that Angelina can't cook either."

"That's all a ruse, something the publicity people came up with to keep the publishers of celebrity cookbooks off Angie's back," said Brad, now letting America in on a long-held secret. "Angie is a tremendous cook and makes the best spaghetti and meatballs dinner I have ever tasted. That's what made my decision. I think a lot of guys are like that."

Over at *Today*, Ann Curry finished her newsbreak about halfway through Diane Sawyer's live interview with the two famed movie stars. Then Ann looked directly into the camera with a big smile on her face and said, "And now, my exclusive interview with Angelina Jolie, taped just a few days ago in Hollywood."

On the screen appeared Ann standing with Angelina in her kitchen in Hollywood, as the brunette movie star dressed in a pink apron, stirred a pan full of red sauce.

"It was always about the sauce," said Angelina. "I go through major preparation to use the freshest tomatoes. And the meatballs, I treat them like they are my children, and you know how much I love my children."

Today thought they had a major scoop showing that Angelina Jolie could actually cook, but they were just a few minutes behind the *GMA* story. The *Today Show* producer, who came out earlier to try and warn Meredith Vieira about the parasailing segment on ABC, came running out of the wings once again. "They have Angelina live on ABC! With Brad Pitt!" she yelled across the set of *Today*. "Live! And Brad says Angelina can cook!"

A close up of a tanned and handsome Brad Pitt was now filling the screen at *GMA* as he provided the details to Diane Sawyer that all of America had waited to hear for years. "Most people think Angie and I had some great sexual affair when we were filming *Mr. & Mrs. Jones*. They thought that I was so intoxicated by her incredible beauty and that I fell in love with her, and then broke up with Jennifer. Well that's not what happened at all. After filming one day, Angie invited me over to her place saying she would make me a wonderful meal. Well, I knew her terrible cooking reputation, so I went, just to be polite. But after eating Angie's Italian dinner that evening, which was incredibly good, I told her I had to have her sauce, her meatballs, the whole thing, and I would leave Jennifer to have it."

Brad dropped his head, then said in a low tone as if he had received an ultimatum he couldn't refuse, "She told me that was fine, and she would serve me Italian at least twice a week, as long as I agreed to adopt half of Southeast Asia and maybe have a few kids of our own. It seemed like a good idea at the time."

Diane finished the segment on that note, a segment that would draw national and international coverage, while the "cooking segment" on *Today* drew a few yawns and another low mark on the media scorecard, which now read: *GMA* 1,156, *Today* –322.

Ken Bowers, who looked more disheveled than usual given the events of the morning, knew what was in front of him if he allowed this to continue. He paced the floor, now determined to win at all costs. "Oh yeah, they think we are licked, do they?" said Bowers, laughing through clenched teeth. "I'll show 'em licked. I'll improvise with stuff they can't copy. They'll have to do better than steal our production plan and schedule to beat me. They want to see a first-rate news program, an Emmy Award winning news program. I'll show 'em!"

He turned to his best segment producer and ordered, "Get that mound of dirt in the storage room, a lot of water, and that big plastic pool we used last year. Mix it all up and make a pool of mud.

"Ann and Meredith, I need you for a how-to segment," he ordered his two attractive news stars in a not-so-nice tone.

"How-to segment? How to what?" asked Ann, still reeling from being beaten on her big exclusive.

"How to mud-wrestle! Get changed into shorts and T-shirt, both of you. I'm winning this ratings period," he said, then turned away to talk into his headset. "Tell Matt Lauer to get on that senior citizens' beach."

In complete shock at the ridiculous request made of them, Ann and Meredith both approached their producer, "Ken, you are kidding, right?"

"No, I'm not kidding!" said the sweaty, red-eyed executive producer, with an angry scowl across his face that belonged in a boxing ring, not a newsroom. "Do you think for one second that I am going to let *Good Morning America* beat me in the ratings? Beat us?"

"But Ken, we are professional journalists, not mud-wrestlers!" said Ann.

"Yes!" Meredith quickly agreed, knowing her executive producer had just lost his mind for a moment. "We don't mud-wrestle in order to get ratings!"

"You don't?" yelped Bowers.

"No!" said the two newswomen in unison.

"Well, I can promise you both, if you aren't ready to mix it up in that mud pit in two minutes, you'll be out of jobs this afternoon."

Meredith and Ann just looked at each other in complete dismay when they saw Kathie Lee Gifford running in from the wings, dressed in Nike shorts and a New York Giants T-shirt. She was followed by *Today*'s weekend anchor Natalie Morales, dressed in a runner's outfit.

"Ken, we're ready to go," said Kathie Lee, huffing and puffing, having run from the newsroom as fast as she could upon hearing the argument in the studio.

"She won't take me down Ken," said Natalie Morales, a good athlete and distance runner. "I'll give her a fight she won't forget. And then I want Meredith's job. Deal?"

"Deal!" said Bowers.

"And I want Ann's job!" demanded Kathie Lee.

"Done! Now that's the kind of spirit I want to see!" proclaimed Bowers, again turning away to talk into his headset. "Is Matt on that beach yet? Good, then let's go to him. Do you have the copy ready? Great! Meredith, when we come back, you do the intro."

"But, I thought you were firing me?" she said with her voice cracking, nearly crying.

"Not yet, I haven't," snapped Bowers.

A devastated Meredith Vieira just looked at her friend Ann wondering who put the tent over the circus in which they were now performing. When the show came back from a commercial break, like the professional she has always been, Meredith read the copy, "And now we are going back to the sandy white beaches of St. Pete where our own Matt Lauer has mistakenly been dropped onto the beach where the Snowbirds convention is taking place. And even worse, he was mistakenly handed a Viagra pill instead of the aspirin he requested for his headache!"

She looked at Bowers, "Wow! You're kidding with this right?"

Matt thought Meredith's sarcasm was directed at him and answered, "Thanks, Meredith," he said, now standing on the beach with his tank top off, hands on hips, and personal fishing tackle on display. "I am a bit embarrassed standing here, uh, how do I say this? Well, let's just say that I've caught the attention of a few of the senior lady sunbathers."

Just then, two eighty-year-old former swimsuit models started walking across the beach in their two-inch high heels toward an excited Matt Lauer.

"Is Willard Scott here?" asked one of high-heeled golden girls with a very playful smile on her face. "We love Willard and his jars of jelly, but you'll do. You're young and hot!"

Bowers signaled Meredith to talk.

"Thanks, Matt, we will check back with you and your girlfriends in a few minutes," she said, biting her lip to deliver the next line. "Now we are going live, in studio here, for a 'How-to segment.' A lot of women want to know just what it is like to mud-wrestle. Is it something they should consider as a workout to lose weight?"

Meredith rolled her eyes and looked at Ann who had her head in her hands trying to block out this zaniness.

"Our own Kathie Lee Gifford and Natalie Morales will square off here to show you just how it's done. Go to it, ladies."

Meredith then dropped the script and walked off the set, followed by Ann, who looked torn by the decision. Beloved weatherman Al Roker decided to stay and watch the match, which was a knock-down, drag-out brawl, with Kathie Lee and Natalie wrestling with every ounce of energy they had at eight o'clock in the morning to try and win the match.

Bowers told Roker to get behind the anchor desk and signaled him to read the teleprompter.

"Good match ladies, lots of good hits there," said the jovial, although somewhat perplexed weatherman, as he watched Ann Curry sprint in from the wings, diving straight out and tackling Kathie Lee into the mud pit like an NFL linebacker. "Hey, great hit Ann! That ought to keep your job. Now we are going to check in with Matt to see how he is doing. Matt?"

A shot of Lauer, surrounded by twenty elderly bikini-clad women, all with large straw hats, sunglasses, and two-inch heels, came on the screen. As he stood there, his eyes grew wide in horror as the large group of snow girls descended upon him, forming a pile no one wanted to see. Out of that pile came a pair of Speedo swimming trunks, once the property of one Matt Lauer.

A wide-eyed Roker watching this scene in amazement asked, "Where in the world is Matt Lauer?"

This last ditch desperate attempt by Bowers failed miserably and *Good Morning America* destroyed *The Today Show* in the ratings for the first time in years. The media coverage from that first day rocketed ABC up to five million viewers and dropped *Today* down to four million, basically a two million viewer swing.

Young Gina Tully knew she had finished a job well done. Someday, maybe, she would let the world in on her secret so interns wouldn't be treated so badly. But that would have to wait for another day. She would go out with a bang though.

After the show had finished, producers were called into crisis meetings all day long, while Gina checked the planning and scheduling log for the week, watching it change after each meeting broke up.

At 2:00 p.m., most of the producers were back at their desks and it looked like the right time for Gina to make her grand exit. She walked into Bowers's office to thank him for the opportunity, but she had contacted Columbia and was told the time she had already put in at *Today* met the requirements for her internship credits and she was leaving that day. A completely stressed-out Bowers, sitting at his computer, stood up from his chair to speak to her outside of his office so everyone in the newsroom could hear, "You go ahead and leave," he yelled, visibly angry. "But let's see you get another station, let alone another network in this country, to hire you. Not without my recommendation! I hope all of you interns heard that. You think you're working for nothing. You're working for our recommendation!"

Gina just laughed, turned to look at everyone in the newsroom and said loudly, "Well Mr. Bowers, I already landed a fulltime paying position at a network. And I did it without your recommendation. So, Mr. Bowers, bye-bye now!'"

After such a challenging day, some in the newsroom couldn't contain their laughter, although they tried ducking under their desks to hide it. So many of them wished they could say the same thing to their lunatic executive producer.

"And by the way, Mr. Bowers," said Tully, prepared to give her parting shot. "The day will come when someone will blow the whistle on guys like you who make staffers do sexually offensive and demeaning segments like mud-wrestling to keep their jobs. And you'll be shown the door!"

"Not in your lifetime honey!" said a smirking Bowers, trying to laugh off the comment.

Gina marched out the door of *The Today Show* for good. A few weeks later on ABC's *World News Tonight*, the newly promoted nightly news anchor, Diane Sawyer, led off a segment about the closing of a snowbird's beach in St. Pete, Florida and threw it to a new reporter for the network, Gina Tully.

"All that remains of a disturbing incident that took place here a few weeks ago are these," said Tully, standing on the beautiful white sand and holding up, at the end of a long stick, a very tattered and torn Speedo swimsuit.

On November 29, 2017, Page Six TV broke the story about Lauer's long history of sexual harassment and he was immediately fired. The next day, Bowers was also fired. *Today Show* staffers who were there during the Sweeps Weeks of November 2008, went out to Morell's Café to celebrate, knowing things were changing for the better in newsrooms across America.

ABOUT THE AUTHOR

John Bernard Ruane is an author, journalist, and PR counselor. He was a feature writer for the *Chicago Sun-Times for* ten years, before going on to contribute articles and columns to the *Chicago Tribune* and *Atlanta-Journal Constitution*. He is a critically-acclaimed author of three books including *The Earl Campbell Story* (ECW Press, 1999), profiling the life of NFL Hall of Fame running back Earl Campbell and his battle with panic disorder; *Parish the Thought* (Simon and Schuster, 2008), an inspirational memoir about growing up Catholic in the 1960s; and *The Wizards of Spin* (Second City Books), satirical fiction with stories about the giants of television news and talk. In addition, having trained at the famed Second City Theater, Ruane wrote four critically acclaimed satirical sketch comedy shows, a rock-musical play, a short film, and television pilot. During college, Ruane was an English major and two-sport athlete at Chicago State University (hockey and baseball) and played center on two college hockey championship teams. Later, he volunteered his time to coaching fifty-two sports teams in youth baseball, fast-pitch softball and basketball over a seventeen-year period. He has been married to his high school sweetheart, Charlotte, since 1982 and they have four wonderful children.